PRAISE FOR NIKKI TURNER

#1 Essence Bestselling author

"Always surprising, Nikki Turner's prose
moves like a Porsche, switching gears from tender
to vicious in an instant."
—50 CENT

"Nikki Turner has once again taken street literature
to the next level, further proving that she is indeed
'The Queen of Hip Hop Fiction.'"
—ZANE, author of *Dear G-Spot*

"Another vivid slice of street life from Nikki Turner. You
can't go wrong with this page-turner!"
—T. I. on *Ghetto Superstar*

"Few writers working in the field today bring
the drama quite as dramatically as Nikki Turner . . .
[She's] a master at weaving juicy, 'hood-rich sagas
of revenge, regret, and redemption."
—Vibe on *Forever a Hustler's Wife*

"USDA hood certified."
—TERI WOODS, author of the True to the Game
trilogy on *Riding Dirty on I-95*

HEARTBREAK OF A HUSTLER'S WIFE

Heartbreak of a Hustler's Wife

A NOVEL

Nikki Turner

ONE WORLD TRADE PAPERBACKS

BALLANTINE BOOKS NEW YORK

Turner

A One World Trade Paperback Original

Copyright © 2011 by Nikki Turner

Published in the United States by One World Books,
an imprint of The Random House Publishing Group,
a division of Random House, Inc., New York.

ONE WORLD is a registered trademark and the One World
colophon is a trademark of Random House, Inc.

LIBRARY OF CONGRESS CATALOGING-IN-PUBLICATION DATA
Turner, Nikki.
Heartbreak of a hustler's wife : a novel / Nikki Turner.
p. cm.
"A One World Trade Paperback original"—T.p. verso.
ISBN 978-0-345-51108-9 (pbk.)—ISBN 978-0-345-52640-3 (ebook)
1. Wives—Fiction. 2. Criminals—Family relationships—Fiction.
3. Street life—Fiction. 4. African Americans—Fiction.
5. Richmond (Va.)—Fiction. 6. Domestic fiction.
7. Urban fiction. I. Title.
PS3620.U7659H43 2011
813'.6—dc22   2011001780

Printed in the United States of America

www.oneworldbooks.net

2 4 6 8 9 7 5 3 1

Book design by Laurie Jewell

*To everyone who asked for this book:
without you this novel would never have
been written! Enjoy!*

A Special Message from
Nikki to Her Readers

Dear Loyal Readers:

As always, I'd like to say thank you for your undying support of my many books and authors, which you have embraced with open minds, hearts, and arms. I feel blessed and honored to have such loyal and faithful readers. That's why when I got email after email after email from you asking for the third segment of the Hustler's Wife series, I didn't hesitate. Now, I'm not going to pretend that writing this book was easy because, like most works of art, it's never a smooth ride. I talked a little about this in the letter I wrote to you in my novel, *Natural Born Hustler,* but there were other bumps in the road too.

In April of last year, while writing this book, I was injured in a car accident, resulting in headaches and back and neck pain, which severely limited the amount of time I could spend writing on the computer. My physical therapist advised me to push the book back—but how could I? Every single spring you've counted on me for a Nikki Turner Original, and letting you down was not an option. So, I soldiered forward slowly and steadily in pain every day. I couldn't take pain pills because they put me to sleep, and with my editor on my back and a follow-up book to write, who had time for sleep? Besides, my grandmother used to tell me that there would be plenty of time to sleep once I'm dead and gone . . . and my heartbeat and aching muscles told me that I was neither dead nor gone. Thank GOD!

But the most dreadful part was when the doctor delivered the heart-wrenching news that due to my sciatic nerve causing the charley horse–like pains in my legs, I should limit myself to wearing only flat shoes. To a female fashionista with a fetish for high-end high heels that news was equivalent to a death sentence, but I'm keeping the hope alive . . .

But those weren't the only impediments I faced: I had a story line that needed to be orchestrated. The characters all wanted their voices to be heard, and it was up to me to weave a great story for them. I wanted an amazing first chapter, which took me three months to write, only for my editor to move it to another part of the book. But I took every little detail about this story seriously because I felt like it was an important turning point, not only in my career as a writer, but for Yarni and Des as characters. They've been through so much more than most relationships could ever hope to survive, and the question for me was: can their love weather this latest storm or is this it for them?

If you enjoy reading this book as much I enjoyed telling the story, then it will be worth the excruciating pain that I experienced behind the scenes. Thank you again from the bottom of my heart and the depths of my soul for your love and support.

Much love,
Nikki

HEARTBREAK OF A HUSTLER'S WIFE

Prologue

"Des, you can't play with God anymore. You just can't." Yarni was adamant.

"This has nothing to do with God. I need to find out who tried to kill me."

"Why isn't it enough that whoever tried wasn't successful? That you are still alive? That you are still able to take your daughter and wife in your arms? It was God who saved your life. It's because of His Grace and mercy that you are not lying in the morgue and that I'm not making funeral arrangements for you."

"That may all be well and true, but what am I supposed to do now? Let it go? I'm not cut from that kind of cloth, Yarni, and you know that. That's not who I am, and you know that's not the person that you married."

"I know that, Des, but are you going to be fifty years old and still popping caps in a nigga's butt?" Seeing that Des wasn't changing his mind, she tried a different line. "But what about evolving?"

"I've evolved. I'm not selling dope."

"No more, you mean. But you're collecting money from it. I just want you to do one or the other."

"What do you mean one or the other?"

Yarni looked him in the eyes "The streets or the pulpit. And preferably anything but the streets. I don't want you to be a hypocrite." She knew her words would hurt him, but hell, right at that moment, the truth was something Des needed to hear.

"Look, I hear you, baby. I really do. But right now, until I figure out who tried to kill me, I guess I'm choosing the streets."

1

The Good Life

Yarni mingled with the congregation of the Good Life Ministry, which was one of her many obligations as first lady of the church. As she looked around at the lavish décor, her heart started to melt. This church was her husband's vision, and if she hadn't known any better, it was something that God had bestowed upon Des.

The transformation from super grocery store to megachurch was spectacular. Everything about the place was nothing less than first class and Des had spared no expense bringing his vision to life. The stained glass windows were imported from Europe, while the hand-crafted padded pews were adorned with intricately carved arms and backrests. There were at least twenty 80-inch plasma television monitors affixed to the walls throughout the sanctuary to assure everyone the experience of virtual front-row seating. The pulpit was a huge stage fit for a Grammy Award–winning artist. To the lower right of the pulpit is where the church musicians assembled. Yarni was proud of what her husband had built, and she was equally ashamed of the blood money that funded it.

For most of his life, her husband, Des, had been a stone-cold hustler, so it didn't amaze Yarni when, three and a half years ago, he came up with the idea to create the Good Life Ministry as a means to make and launder money. He had realized that the dope game was becoming a game for suckers. Des was sure he had it all figured out: churches didn't have to pay taxes and there was no way to monitor how much money they took in. People were lost and confused and needed answers about why things in the world and their communities were as messed up as they were. Once Des witnessed an ordained, Bible-toting pastor pimp the pulpit at his nephew's funeral, he was convinced that the church game wasn't difficult. All one needed was a fresh pair of gators, a few scriptures under their belt and a hell of a talk game. Well, Des had two of the three on lockdown, and learning the Bible inside and out didn't take him long at all.

In the beginning, Yarni didn't approve and was furious about Des making a mockery of people's faith, but she eventually realized her opinion wasn't going to change his mind. So she repented every day for her husband's sins and made Des promise to do good by the church if he insisted on going through with his unholy plan. As always, he exceeded her expectations. He took the devil's money and shared it with God's people, becoming a blessing to all those in need. He paid bills for those who had gotten behind, bought air conditioners for the elderly in the summer, school supplies for the kids, made Thanksgiving and Christmas jump off for the less fortunate, sponsored summer trips for the kids, donated trucks of food and offered 24-hour child care for working mothers. On top of all that, he even built housing for the homeless. His example of giving was outstanding, and his rapidly growing congregation respected and loved him for his contributions to the underdog. He made the Good Life Ministry a necessity, a movement, where they took care of their own and the neighborhood.

The ex-junkies and drug dealers could relate to him. They understood, adored and cheered him on. They weren't fooled into believing he was a reborn saint nor did he ever try to swindle them into thinking that. He had simply shared his past, his testimony, with the people. Just in case anybody tried to dig up unturned dirt on him, he'd practically handed them the shovel. The fewer secrets a man has . . . the less likely a chance of those secrets being revealed.

Des was the first to admit he wasn't an angel who had fallen down from Heaven. But what made him stand out from other preachers was that he was giving at a time when everyone else seemed to be taking. That made him a savior in his sheep's eyes.

A third of the congregation was made up of older members. The elderly people had joined Des's church because it reminded them of the old days when a neighborhood church actually stood for something. Most new churches seemed to start out in the hood, but as soon as the going got good, they started a building fund to move the church as far away as they could. Des had no intentions of uprooting his ministry. The hood was where it was at.

The laid-back, come-as-you-are atmosphere of the largest ministry south of the James River welcomed all races, religions and lifestyles. The message was inclusiveness, and the practice was giving. The leaders and congregation prayed for God to bless them so abundantly that they'd be a blessing to someone else. From housewife to prostitute to professional—all were welcome with open arms, and many accepted the invitation to praise life . . . the Good Life.

"That dress you're wearing is off the chain." Yarni turned to find out where the compliment was coming from and spied a smiling twenty-something-year-old girl. She was one of the newer members. "I hope I'm not being too intrusive by asking where you got that bad mam-ma-jama."

Yarni thought the girl was attractive in a stripper sort of way with her high heels and tight-fitting skirt. She recalled having spoken to her once or twice before, but for the life of her, she couldn't remember the girl's name. *Rebecca? Rosetta? Rhonda? Rosalyn? Robin?* She tried to recollect but kept coming up empty.

The girl stood out because every single time Yarni saw her at the church, she was attached to the arm of a different older man. However, on this particular day, the guy she was playing arm candy to was a little younger than the others had been. There was one thing Yarni could give props to when it came to the young woman's suitors: each and every one of them was always as clean as a first-rate operating room. The smug-looking fella she was with this Sunday wore a dark, nicely cut suit, cashmere overcoat and a black fedora angled low over his eyes.

"Thank you very much," Yarni said graciously. "It wouldn't

be a bother at all. Actually, a good friend of mine from New York made it. She also designed the one Desi is wearing."

The girl's eyes shot to Yarni's daughter, little Desi, who as if on cue with the cutest snaggle-toothed smile gave a half twirl, side to side, and a curtsey to better model the outfit.

"Oh she's so adorable and such a little lady," the young lady cooed.

"Thank you," Desi said. The child beamed, beating her mother to the punch before Yarni could accept the compliment on her behalf.

Yarni smiled at Desi and then at the nameless promiscuously dressed hootchie and said, "The next time we run into each other, I'll try to have the designer's number for you. And hopefully that'll be next Sunday. You will be back to fellowship with us, won't you?"

"By all means," the young lady assured her.

"For now, though, I'm sure Des has a right-on-time word to give this Sunday. So welcome and thank you and your guest for coming. We're so happy to have you here."

The nameless hootchie thanked Yarni and then worked her four-inch heels across the glass-polished floor of the open foyer to take her seat with the new fella. Yarni continued to share small talk and pleasantries with a few other church members until she saw the musicians taking their places. That was her cue to take her designated seat on the fifth row behind the deacons and deaconess.

As soon as she was seated, the choir began to take their places around the church in preparation for a grand entrance. The mass choir had been putting it down since Des formed the Good Life Ministry. Everyone expected them to set the atmosphere with their anointed gift to sing praises unto the Lord. In fact, a lot of the devoted congregation mostly came to hear them perform.

When the musicians cued up, all movement and talking ceased, and the choir started to enter. They wore beautiful green and gold robes with the letters *GLM* embossed along the left side.

Yarni thought about the conversation she and Des had had that morning.

$ $ $

"Just remember, Des, you are playing a dangerous game, not just with the people of the church, but with God. And know, God can be your best friend or your worst enemy!"

Yarni could see in Des's face that her words tore at him like daggers. For a single instant she thought they just might be the words to give him the change of heart she so much desired for him to have. But her hope was short-lived when Des replied, "All your prayers are accepted and appreciated. So pray for me."

"I always do."

"A'ight, look," he took a deep breath as if he was trying to cleanse all of the uncertainty he may have felt, "I'm going to fall back off the church until I can figure out what's really going on and how I'm going to deal with it."

"And you have to promise me that you are going to do some soul searching about this church. I know it might sound crazy, Des, but maybe God used the streets to get you into the church.

I mean, honey, there's no denying that you're good at leading," she encouraged him. "When you are in that pulpit giving the word, it's like you're in your element—your true element."

Des cracked a smile as Yarni continued. "And I believe that God has really been working on you, but I honestly don't want you to get back in that pulpit until you figure out if you are going to be real with God or not."

Des wished she'd just let sleeping dogs lie, because know he wasn't feeling where Yarni was going with this whole thing. Him, a man of the cloth? For real? Wasn't gon happen. That very thought showed on his face and it wasn't hard for Yarni to detect.

"Look, all I'm saying is God has been with you all this time, watching over you and keeping you clean of all the dirt. His patience is going to run out. He's blessing you now but if you don't get it right, He can curse you too."

"The book says God watches out for fools and babies . . . and I'm neither," Des continued.

$ $ $

The lead vocalist brought Yarni back to the present. She had the kind of voice that reached out, grabbed everyone by the collar and demanded their attention. Yarni started rocking her head as the choir backed the vocalist by singing, "God will work it out," in perfect harmony. The moment was bittersweet for Yarni. Her eyes glistened behind salty tears.

2

Motivation

The church musicians switched gears to an instrumental. The man performing on the keyboard and the drummer were both banging their hearts out while the lead guitar and bass players battled for supremacy in their own private competition. But when the sax player added his harmonic flavor, he nearly stole the show.

Now it was time.

Des entered the sanctuary as if he had his very own theme music.

The musicians and choir may have been the reason many of the seats were filled, but make no mistake about it: Des was the superstar and the stage belonged to him.

He came gliding down the middle aisle bopping his freshly cut head full of wavyhair to the uplifting beat. So smooth, he could've been walking on water. He wore a dark green four-button custom-made suit, a tailored French-cuff gold shirt and string-up gators so fresh that if he slipped them off they might've tried to take refuge in the nearest marsh. In the pulpit, he took his seat in a huge high-back gold and money green velvet chair, fit for a king.

As the soloist broke down the tempo, the music heightened. Once the song ran its course, having brought the congregation to a state of complete worship, the lead soloist handed the mic over to Des. With the mic in the shepherd's hands, the volume of the music was lowered. Des descended from his throne and stepped up to the podium. Everyone looked at him like he was E. F. Hutton: when he spoke, people listened.

Looking out into the sea of faces, he spoke into an invisible mic, "It looks like everybody made it safely from the clubs last night, huh?" Half the crowd laughed because there was quite a bit of truth buried in the humor. That was the half who liked the afternoon service most; they could party all night, sleep the buzz off and still get their praise on without the liquor odor seeping out of their pores. Morning services didn't accommodate such a lifestyle.

"Yeah, some of y'all looking like, 'Not me!' Yes, you. It's all good, though. No offense intended." He looked upon the congregation with a serious face. "But that's between you and God. I'm not here to judge you, embarrass you, or call you out. I'm just here to tell you what saith the Lord." Des could see he was getting a reaction; as usual it fueled him to press on. "Y'all know how I do it. I'ma speak it like I see it, and if it don't apply to you, then let it fly. Ya feel me? In other words, let the church say, 'Amen.'"

Amens rang throughout the sanctuary.

Yarni marveled at how Des lit up the already bright room with his trademark smile. After all, this was the same youthful smile and quick wit that Yarni had fallen in love with so many years ago. She blew him a kiss. No one noticed. Every single eye was glued to the preacher man. Des tossed a look back to his wife that said, "I love you."

When she caught it, they both smiled. Des continued to mes-merize the congregation while Yarni sat in awe of her man's fi-nesse. But not long into the service, something didn't feel right to her. She scanned the church, but nothing or no one looked out of place. Unable to put her finger on why she suddenly felt that way, she tried to put her focus back on Des's words, but as hard as she tried, she could not ignore the bad feeling churning in the pit of her stomach.

She tried to maintain eye contact with Des while he gave a phenomenally inspirational message on why financial literacy and spiritual literacy were equally necessary in the community. The room was pin-drop silent as the people took in every word he said. If Des knew anything, it was that folks always paid at-tention when it came to talking about money. Finance was one of Des's favorite subjects, and with the economy struggling the way it was, his followers loved hearing about how to get their hands on the almighty dollar now more than ever. Des had everyone's attention, with some even taking notes. Most of the deacons were even intrigued, but not Slim; he was too busy on his job as the main lookout, making sure nothing around him looked or got out of order.

There were well over fifty deacons on board; all good men, for the most part, but Des only trusted six with specific tasks.

His friendship went back more than three decades with most of those men. Tony, Black Bob, Chip, Mo, Stanka and Slim were Des's road dogs.

Tony and Black Bob were brothers: Tony was younger and the more ambitious and reckless of the two. Chip was a bookworm and a genius with a computer. He should've graduated from MIT, but he got arrested for creating a high-stakes pyramid scam his freshman year. Nobody could remember a time when Des and Slim weren't down for each other. Stanka, Yarni's uncle, proved to be a real stand-up brotha. And the fact that he would do anything for Yarni was enough to win Des over. Mo was the most physically intimidating of the crew. He was huge, with muscles growing out of muscles. Des got tight with him after a riot in prison. All of his trusted crew packed concealed, sixteen-shot .40 caliber Glocks under their suit jackets, but Slim was the top man and the leader of the pack.

$ $ $

That morning at a meeting before the first service, Des gave strict instructions to his crew.

"Everyone needs to be extra-vigilant at all the services," Des explained.

Tony nodded. "What we looking for?"

"I'm not sure, but if the Holy Ghost step up in this piece and it don't look right, I need y'all on top of it. I got a funny feeling about today. And y'all know how I am when my sixth sense kicks in? It's nothing concrete, but I'd rather waste time being safe than run out of time because I wasn't."

$ $ $

Now, several hours later, Des was heavy into his sermon. As he philosophized the word, he was careful to make periodic eye contact with each of his top men. The crew trusted Des's instincts. If the weatherman said it was going to be sunny and Des said it felt like rain, they packed umbrellas along with their gats. Better safe than sorry.

A few minutes later, while Des was explaining his ideology of assets and liabilities, seven brothers in black suits and long over-coats stood up from the pews, at first blending in with everyone else, on their feet cheering Des on with applause and Amens. Before anybody saw it coming, the coats flew open, and all seven drew guns. Sleek and compact MP5s, which had been concealed as well as a flask in the inside pocket of a casual fan at a football game. In the blink of an eye the machine guns were out, front and center.

Slim was one of the first of the deacons to peep the game, but he hadn't spotted it soon enough. He thought about snatching the Glock from the shoulder holster underneath his jacket but knew better. The automatic weapons the men had brazenly brandished were capable of spitting more than five hundred rounds per minute. He knew his pistol wouldn't stand a chance up against that type of firepower.

One of the gunmen spoke up. He must have been in charge. "Y'all here, sinners and saints alike, know what's up. This here is a robbery. For those of you who only speak church language: it's offering time!"

And in harmony, his partners hummed the line from the old

classic Eazy-E song "Nobody Move, Nobody Get Hurt." And if that wasn't bizarre enough, these exact words appeared on all the TV monitors throughout the church.

"What the fuck is going on?" a member of the Good Life Ministry called out. He was an older man. A former drug dealer. Before anyone could react, one of the gunmen caught him with a cold blow right upside the dome.

"Okay, people, don't make this motherfucking shit any more *got-damn* complicated than this shit has to be," the gunman in charge of the mission advised.

Some members of the congregation weren't close enough to hear what he said, but everyone was close enough to one of the guys pointing the menacing weapons to understand that they should cooperate. Or die.

Tony went for his gun. With less effort than it takes to snap a finger to a catchy tune, the gunman nearest him tapped the trigger. Surprisingly, there was little sound. The silent slug snatched Tony from his feet, sending him to the shiny polished wood floor with blood pouring from his chest.

"Now, he was a dumb motherfucker!" The gunman that had pulled the trigger went over to Tony and kicked him. "Don't you be like this idiot." He pointed the MP5 machine gun in an arcing motion to emphasize his point. The other members of the congregation looked on with a tangled mixture of fear, shock and worry.

Sister Mary, who was an elder of the congregation and acted as a great-grandmother to most in the church, stood up boldly, unafraid of the hoodlums. She pointed a bony index finger at the gunman, her face twisted with anger and defiance. "You going straight to Hell, coming in here taking from the people of God. You gon rot in Hell." She spoke with conviction, matching the gunman's stare beat for beat.

He responded by aiming his gun at her head. "Sit the *fuck* down, Grandma, before you drop more than your money. Yeah, I may lose my soul over this, but you, old biddy, you might lose your life. So take off the Superwoman cape, put on your prayer shawl and pray to your God that I don't take you out of your misery."

She cut him a look that only a no-nonsense grandmother from the South could deliver. Sister Mary hadn't gotten to her age by being a fool. She followed the gunman's instructions and sat down. Under her breath, she uttered, "You still going to Hell." She rolled her eyes and added, "Crumb snatchchas."

There was no way Des could let something like this go without retribution. He had a reputation to uphold: not only was God watching, but so were the streets. And the streets were watching from row seats and pews alike. He was tempted to reach for his own automatic weapon stashed under the podium and begin gunning himself, but there were too many innocent lives involved. Especially his wife and daughter. He noticed that Yarni had put their daughter underneath the pew to protect her as best she could under the unorthodox circumstances.

Sometimes diplomacy was the best course of action, he thought.

Into his microphone, Des spoke for the first time since the potentially deadly interruption started. "Please, my brothers and sisters, don't do anything rash. I'll personally replace any- and everything that these people take. You have my word." Des would rather die like a man than live like a coward. He knew what he wanted to do, but there was no need to risk the lives of so many over money. "With the power of God, saints, you will be restored."

Des and the leader of the gunmen locked eyes, which had nothing to do with one trying to intimidate the other; they were simply conveying a message to each other in a telepathic, psychological gangsta language that they both seemed to understand.

The gunman's look said, "Chalk it up as a loss. It's just part of the game."

While Des's look said, "There's a consequence behind every action. I hope you can handle it when it's reciprocated."

Trash bags were quickly passed throughout each and every aisle and were gradually filled with wallets, credit cards and jewelry. Sister Mary continued to spew contemptuous venom. "Robbing old ladies' purses. It don't make no sense. The fire of Hell y'all going to feel."

Long after the bold gunmen were gone, Des figured out that the whole thing had all been staged to divert attention from the real heist. While everyone in the sanctuary was emptying their pockets, two other gunmen had overtaken Chip, the church's accountant, in the back office and forced him to wire ten million dollars to an overseas account. The move was brilliant, Des had to admit to himself. Except for one thing. They had definitely fucked with the wrong preacher's money.

In the Media

Later on that day, Des was interviewed at home by the police, who took a report of the shooting. Once the officers were gone, Des went to make a stiff drink for Slim and himself.

Slim felt tired. He'd barely slept since Des was shot at on Friday, and with the robbery today, he was exhausted. He took a seat on the sofa and began to flip through the channels on the oversized high-definition flat-screen television that was mounted on the wall. He turned up the volume when he saw a news reporter on the front steps of the church. "Yo, look, Des," he called out. "Hurry up, man!"

"The Good Life Ministry has a growing membership and is known for the good deeds it performs throughout the community. It is actually becoming a force to be reckoned with in Richmond. But today it turned into a set from a real-life gangster movie when armed robbers came into the place of worship and killed two men while holding the entire church at gunpoint.

"The would-be holy heisters made off with jewelry, cash and other valuables from the congregation before the police arrived on the scene. Leads are sketchy and the minister, Desmond Taylor, could not be reached for comment. However, outraged members had plenty to say about the heist."

The camera went onto location and Sister Mary was the first person they showed. Still dressed in her Sunday best, she looked into the camera and said her piece. "The people who did this are going to go straight to Hell. Aside from that, I feel sorry for what God is going to do to them." The reporter tried to pull the microphone away from her; Sister Mary wasn't having it. She arm-wrestled the reporter, won and brought the microphone closer to her mouth. "I'm not finished yet," she told him, giving the young reporter the same look she'd shot at the thug who had threatened her life.

"They got some nerve coming into the house of the *Lord* and taking not only from *God's* people but from *God's* tithes and offerings. It ain't about the people. It ain't about our loss. It's about His harvest! God's harvest." She pointed at the church. "You know the Bible says those who steal from God will be cursed." Sister Mary rolled on with conviction now that she had the stage. "Now, that ain't no hogwash that some Bible-toting man made up. That's what the good book says." She nodded and kept going. "And those men—I feel pity on what *God* gonna do to them. May He have mercy on their rotten souls."

The reporter had heard enough from Sister Mary and motioned for the cameraman to cut to another bystander. "They going to Hell with gasoline drawers on," the young man stated to the camera.

The reporter switched gears. "Do you know about the rumors of the supposedly street-reformed minister of this church still being involved in the drug world? Do you think there is any truth to the speculation that this was drug-related? Perhaps a past debt owed? Or even a current debt, for that matter?" Judging by the reporter's face, he looked as though he felt he'd hit the jackpot with this line of questioning. One didn't move up in this field by asking soft questions.

"Naw, Des been out of the game and he's rich in his own right. Before he even started this church he had an expensive car lot. Why would he still be throwing bricks, man?" The younger member flipped the script, twisting up his mug. "And why is the first thing you people think when a black man is getting money is that he's selling dope?" They quickly took the camera off the young man, hoping to get a different perspective from another church member.

"Naw, it's related to this economy and people doing bad," a middle-aged lady answered the reporter's question. "People see us eating, doing well at the Good Life Ministry, and they want to take from our plates." The woman was nicely dressed. She paused to pat her head to make sure every hair was in place and then looked directly into the camera. "But like our Pastor Taylor says, we going to pray for our enemies. And *God* will deal with them."

Bound and determined to keep digging for dirt, the reporter looked to a bystander with purple hair that matched her purse and nail polish, hoping she would embarrass herself and the minister. "Do you think this had anything to do with the past criminal life he lived?"

"Heck naw," the girl exclaimed. "That man been left that life alone. He's a living witness that people can change. He's given his life to *God*. This ain't no joke. He da real deal. And if anybody wanna get their hair done, you can come see me at Hair Extremes on Jeff Davis Highway."

"Do you know how much was stolen?" the reporter asked a lady who had a mouthful of gold teeth and a rat-tail comb stuck in the back of her hair.

"Well, they only got a few dollars from me because I learned at a young age to keep my money where nobody can find it." The lady then went into her bosom and removed a small bundle of cash.

"Do she even go to the church?" Des asked, handing Slim his drink.

"I never saw her," Slim replied, shaking his head. "But your people held you down. Nobody had a negative word to say about you."

"For sure," Des agreed. "Not that any of them would have anything on me. Turn that shit off, I've seen enough."

Slim was about to turn the television off when Detective Columbo popped up on the screen, preparing to make a statement. This, they both wanted to hear.

"We are looking for the assailants and we will catch them," Columbo stated. "But unofficially, it is still unclear if this is a retaliation based on Mr. Taylor's past as a drug dealer. Whatever the case, I assure you that the Richmond Police Department, in conjunction with the state police, will get to the bottom of it,"

Columbo finalized his tough-stance words with a nod and a false smile for the television camera.

Slim hit the off button on the remote and took a hard swallow of his cognac. "This shit is already getting out of control."

"Tell me something I don't know." Des, still in disbelief, sat down next to Yarni on the couch. "On Friday a sniper took a shot at me and two days later everybody in my church is robbed at gunpoint and my bank account is ten mil lighter. To top all that shit off, Tony is dead." Des shook his head. "Damn." He couldn't believe his boy was gone.

"It was no less than nine to ten people down with the robbery," Slim surmised. "At least that's what I counted. But I believe there had to be others behind the scenes. It's almost impossible for that many people to keep something this big a secret. The streets are going to bust that one wide open for us. It's just a matter of time." Slim swallowed. He took a deep breath. Exhaled. "I'm more concerned about who tried to put the slug from a high-powered rifle through your heart. That shit seemed a lot more professional, if you ask me."

"You might have a point there, man," Des had to agree. "I still can't believe how lucky I was a Bible saved my life." All of their eyes rested on the book that sat on the table. Des kept it in plain view as a reminder of how his life had been spared.

"Luck had nothing to do with it," Yarni said. She'd given him the small customized Bible as a present, and for no explainable reason Des had placed it into the inside pocket of his coat moments before the shot was fired. If the Bible hadn't absorbed the impact, he would've been dead. The bullet itself was still embedded in the pages. "It was more like divine intervention."

4

Like Father, Like Daughter

A few days later, Yarni's mother, Gloria, dropped an atomic bomb on her. "What did you say?" Yarni said into the phone. She was sitting on the bench at the foot of her bed.

"My biopsy came back," Gloria repeated, "and they're saying that they found some cancer cells."

This can't be happening, Yarni thought. "Did you get a second opinion?"

"Yes, and a third." Gloria's voice sounded strong, but worried.

Yarni's mother had always been her rock. Gloria had been there for Yarni through thick and thin, when she was at her best and even more so when she was at her worst. It was Gloria's strength that had always kept Yarni strong.

"Mommy, I'm here for you and you know that we will get

through this together." Though tears rolled down her cheeks, Yarni tried to hold back her sobs as she comforted her mother. She had relied on her mother for so much over the years, and she was ready to step up and be Gloria's source of support.

"I know we will, baby. There's no doubt in my mind. I've already consulted some of the best doctors Florida has to offer."

"Mommy, you know money is no problem. I'll go in debt if need be, so don't hesitate for a minute to ask if you need anything."

"I know." Gloria sounded like she was handling her diagnosis better than her daughter. "I'm confident in the doctors I'm working with. They're gonna take good care of your momma, girl."

"I think you should come stay with us. At a time like this, you should be with family." It had been seven years since Gloria had moved away to Florida and started her restaurant franchise.

Gloria objected to the idea immediately. "My doctors, husband and business are all here." Yarni knew her mother and could sense that there was something she wasn't telling her.

"We have doctors here, and Sam can come with you. With all the technology at hand, he can work from anywhere. And as far as your business, you have people in place that can run the restaurants."

Gloria was adamant, not willing to budge.

"Thanks for the offer, but I'll be just fine, baby. Don't worry."

"Mom, this is crazy for you to have to go through alone."

"I'm not alone. Sam's here."

"I mean, without me. You shouldn't be going through this without me."

"I'm trying to figure out who needs who more here," Gloria sighed, "with everything going on in your life."

"I do need you, Mom, which is why I want to make sure you're here on Earth for as long as possible."

Usually Yarni told Gloria everything. She wanted to share what was going on in her and Des's life with the robbery and all, but this one time she kept her own problems to herself.

Just then the bedroom intercom came to life with Des's voice. "Baby girl, I need you to come down here."

Yarni responded, "I'll be down in a minute."

"Go see what your husband needs. I'll be fine. Baby, don't worry, everything will be okay." Gloria tried to sound convincing, but Yarni could hear the uncertainty in her mother's voice. "We can finish this debate later. Go check on Des."

Yarni didn't want to hang up, but before she could protest, her mother had already told her that she loved her and said good-bye. Gloria had hung up the phone.

Yarni was devastated about her mother's biopsy results. It's all she thought about as she walked down the stairs to be by her man's side.

"It's called covering my ass," Des explained to Slim as Yarni walked into the great room. "I plan on the po-po not givin' a fuck and doing nothing. But if somewhere down the line I have to rubber-band a cat and they find him stretched out, I can say I was in fear for my life. And to better my defense, I would have already created the paper trail to back me up when I'm facing those twelve on the jury." Des turned and winked at Yarni, letting her know that he's paid attention to her work.

Yarni rolled her eyes. Des was always finding a way to make

things work in his favor. His own favor, mind you. This had nothing to do with the favor of God.

Putting dirt in the face of the person responsible would come naturally, Des thought, but first they had to find out who the person or people were who were fucking with his life and livelihood. It was like trying to figure out when a prostitute contracted HIV: the possibilities were endless.

Des had put his hands on over a million dollars before his eighteenth birthday. Being from the hood in the eighties with that type of cake behind a man's mitt brings lots of enemies. And the list didn't end with his foes. If Yarni wouldn't have run across the paperwork naming his boy, Rico, as a federal witness against Des in a CCE case, Des never would have believed it. Rico was his street brother, loyalty bound by blood. Betrayal of that loyalty cost Rico his life. Could Rico's Colombian family be out for retribution? They definitely had the money and the resources. And everyone knows that on the streets, the desire for revenge often never goes away. Like a family gene, it's passed on from one generation to the next.

"I'ma get a shower and some rest," Des said to Slim. "Think about this shit some more. Hit me if something comes up before morning, a'ight? Besides, I think Yarni and I need some alone time."

Slim understood. He gave Des a pound and a brotherly hug and hugged Yarni before leaving.

Yarni and Des, worn out both physically and mentally from the past days' events, retreated up the stairs. In the master bathroom, hot water pelted Des from all directions in the shower. The multiple-positioned shower sprayers were earning the mint he'd put out to have them installed. He soaped up his hand and slid it across the large bruise on the left side of his chest from the impact of the bullet that unsuccessfully tried to take him out a few days ago. He silently thanked God.

Yarni was sitting crossed-legged on the bed, netbook on her lap, when Des walked into the bedroom still dripping from his shower. She was wearing a black negligee that rode high up her well-toned thighs. Desi was asleep in the nursery.

"Don't that thing burn your legs sitting on you like that?" he asked.

Yarni didn't reply. She was too focused on the information on the screen. "Huh? What? Did you say something, honey?" she asked, realizing that Des was not only out of the shower and standing in their bedroom, but that he'd just asked her a question.

"I said, doesn't that thing burn your legs?" He nodded toward the netbook.

"Oh, no, it's fine. That is the least of my worries right now."

Yarni hadn't yet shared her mother's bad news with Des. "Gloria has breast cancer. She just told me about it this evening." Yarni's eyes were still glued to the 9-inch LED screen while she spoke. She'd been Googling information on the disease.

Des, who was putting on his pajamas, paused in mid-action. "Damn, baby, I'm so sorry to hear that. I—is there anything I can do?" Des felt horrible for not noticing that something was wrong. He was so caught up in his own mayhem, he hadn't paid Yarni much attention since he came in.

"Not right now. I asked her to come back to Virginia, maybe move in with us, to be closer to family."

"Good idea," Des agreed. He loved his mother-in-law; she was the one that had come up with the information that was ultimately used as leverage to get him out of prison.

"Yeah, but she turned me down." When Yarni looked at Des, she saw something else on his face besides concern for her mother. "What's on your mind? Is there something I need to know?"

"You mean besides getting shot and the church being robbed?" he joked.

The slight hesitation and uneasy glimmer in his eyes confirmed Yarni's suspicion.

"Okay, baby, what is it? Spit it out and get it over with." She looked at him skeptically.

"My mother told me that I may have another child."

"Come again?" Yarni put her hand up to her ear. "I don't think I heard you correctly."

"Look, I am just as surprised as you are."

"I've never known you to be stupid, Des, so don't play now. The only way you may have a child, as you put it, is if you've been putting your dick where it doesn't belong. Or you somehow got the millennium Virgin Mary pregnant." Yarni was floored. Not in a million years would she have expected this.

"It's not like it sounds, baby."

"Then how is it, Des?" she mocked. "Just tell me exactly how it is."

He began to tell her everything he knew. "The child is eighteen years old. I kicked it with her mother in North Carolina before I ever met you. I never even knew this kid existed until this evening."

Yarni sat outdone as he told her how the child's mother must have kept contact with his mother, Joyce, but made her promise not to tell him about the possibility that he was a father—until now.

Yarni interrupted Des's explanation as if she was making an objection in court. "And your mother just kept this secret to herself?" Before he could respond, Yarni further dissected his excuse. "When has Joyce ever held her mouth closed long enough to keep a secret? When, Des? Really, when has she ever kept a secret? Tell me one time?" She put her finger up. "Oh, but I keep forgetting that when it comes to her family, the secrets are endless. As a matter of fact, that shit is like the Mafia."

Yarni was getting so worked up Des cut her off. "Look, baby, I'm just finding out about this too. I'm just as surprised as you are. I came in the room earlier to tell you as soon as I got off the phone with my mom, but you looked like you were having a pretty intense conversation with your own mother. And then the police came. After Slim left we came up here. You went and got Desi ready for bed. And I took a shower." Des threw his hands up. "This is the first time I've really gotten a chance to talk to you."

"The story is not quite making sense to me. I understand me and your mother don't always see eye to eye, but why now?" she wanted to know. "Why tell us now? Why not eighteen years ago? Why today?"

"The girl's boyfriend got himself shot up and her mother thinks she may be in some type of trouble and someone might be trying to kill her."

"Well, damn, ain't that a chip off of the old block? Like father, like daughter, huh?" she quipped.

Des ignored the sarcasm coming from his wife. "Her mother thought it would be wise to get her out of town for a while," Des explained. "Baby," he reached out and took her hand in his, "I really don't know if this kid is mine or not. That's the truth." He shrugged his shoulders. "But she could be."

"What's her name?" Yarni asked, thinking how could this be happening?

"Desember," he said. "That's what my mother told me. But there's something else."

"How can you possibly top that?" Yarni asked.

"My mom is with her now and is driving her back here. She will be arriving in town tomorrow, and I said that she could stay here with us."

With her hands on her hips, Yarni shook her head. "Well, got-damn, when it rains it pours. I just hope your ass took out flood insurance."

5

What's Done in the Dark . . .
Will Come to the Light

The recent declining state of the economy pounded the stock market almost into submission while the housing market was buckling at the knees. And employment was harder to come by than the highly coveted seats at President Barack Obama's inauguration in Washington, D.C. The prices at the local supermarket were through the roof.

Strange as it may seem, through all of this financial uncertainty, the murder rate in Richmond, Virginia—a city that was once known for one of the highest homicide rates in the country—had also plummeted, to a fraction of the reckless and lawless bloodbath numbers it had a history of putting up in the nineties. In fact crime as a whole was down. It was enough to make some people wonder: if the crime rate was declining in the city, then how come the rate of people going to prison was at an all-time high? The state of Virginia, in conjunction with the U.S. government, spent upward of three hundred million dollars on a brand-new state-of-the-art Federal court facility amongst blighted storefronts and struggling businesses on Broad Street in downtown Richmond. If the deficit had swelled to astronomical figures, trying to revitalize the economy, why would this type of money be wasted on such a grand piece of architecture that wasn't needed? It may not pay to break the law, but it's a known fact that crime paid, and it paid well. And as long as they were building courts, Yarnise Pitman-Taylor, Esquire, would always have employment.

All hell had broken loose in Yarni's personal life, and while a part of her wished she could crawl under a rock and hide, that wasn't the reality of the superwoman that she was.

Des had promised his congregation that he'd make everything all right, that he'd make them whole again, which meant he'd replace whatever was stolen. If Des was nothing else, he was a man of his word. The church had an insurance policy, but there was no telling what it would and wouldn't pay. Whatever the case, Yarni knew this incident could possibly send them into the poor house, but she wasn't going to let that happen if she could help it. So she was ready to pitch in by taking on a day of saving the world and her clients.

The lobby of the circuit court building was brimming with activity as folks of all walks of life—hustlers, prostitutes, robbers, pedophiles, lawyers, police and any- and everything in between—filled the open space. "No cell phones, cameras, Bluetooths, Ipods, combs, brushes, nail files or clippers or any-

thing of that sort is allowed inside this building! If you have
these items take them back to your car now!" Deputy McCall
made the routine announcement in a firm, clear, no-nonsense
voice. A twenty-year veteran of the sheriff's department, he'd
been at John Marshall Courts Building for the past twelve years.

"Make two lines," he continued after observing a few people
pat their pockets, turn and walk out with frustrated grimaces
just thinking about having to go back out in the below-freezing
temperatures. "One in front of each of the two X-ray machines,
and place everything in your pockets into the tray when it's your
turn."

Yarni, bundled up in a long full-length fur coat glided past
the two long lines. With the swagger of a woman who was
clearly used to VIP treatment, she walked straight to the express
lane that was designated for court workers, police officers and at-
torneys. McCall's voice instantly transformed from stern to familiar and polite. "How are you this morning, Mrs. Taylor? Cold
enough for you yet?"

Yarni couldn't help noticing his toothy smile, dingy from
years of smoking. She removed her butter-soft, calf-skin gloves,
revealing her perfectly manicured minx nails. "I'm doing fine,
Fred," she said, "thanks for asking. It's plenty cold all right. So
cold I wasn't sure if I should wear my boots or my ice skates this
morning." The two of them shared a slight chuckle, but Yarni
kept it moving because she was running late. Traffic had been
ridiculous and the clock was working against her this particular
morning. The line for the elevator was at least two loads deep, so
Yarni used her time wisely, since she didn't have much to spare.
She took the steps.

Not many people had believed she could achieve the level of success that she had. With her own checkered past it was only by the grace of God and a lot of hard work that Yarni was a working member of the judicial system. Who could have imagined? After all of the trials, tribulations, perils and pitfalls, cat fights and tightropes that Yarnise Pitman-Taylor had been through that she would have made it to this stage in life?

Like the R&B singer Monica, she was still standing. She had definitely come a long way, she thought as she ascended the two small flights of steps to reach the bull pen where her client was being held until she saw the judge. Lawyers had to log their names and times before being allowed to the holding area.

"Hey, Riley," Yarni said to the deputy sitting at the small desk. "How are you? I need to see Tangaleena Londers."

Riley took a glance at his watch and reluctantly shook his head. "It's a few minutes past cut-off time and my boss is back there. I would if I could."

"I understand," Yarni conceded, knowing that his hands were tied. But she was in a tight spot because this was her first opportunity to speak with her newest client. Yarni had taken the case at the last minute, after receiving a desperate-sounding phone call from the client's mother. Mrs. Londers didn't have many details about the actual crime to pass along to Yarni, but she knew that the magistrate had refused to give her daughter bail. After Yarni agreed to take on the case, it seemed as if within minutes Mrs. Londers had arrived with a portion of the retainer fee.

"I hate being unprepared." Yarni sighed, putting her notes in her purse while Riley looked at his own.

"Well, Mrs. Taylor, it's only a bond hearing it says here. You can handle that. It's a piece of cake for a seasoned attorney like you," he said with an assuring smile.

The compliment brought a smile to her face; still, she was disappointed. "But I don't like taking anything for granted. If you don't mind, let her know that I'm here and they will be calling us shortly."

"Anything for you." Riley winked.

Yarni pushed up one more flight of stairs to the lobby of the third-floor courtroom. She caught sight of Tangaleena's mother in her work uniform, pacing back and forth.

"Hi, Mrs. Londers." Yarni reached out to shake the woman's hand. "I'm glad you could make it." Mrs. Londers's palms were moist from nervous perspiration.

"Yes, of course. I would never miss something this important. I know it looks good for the judge to see that she has a mother who loves her and cares enough to be here for her. I'm waiting for Dougie, that's Tangi's guy friend. He's said he was going to be here early to bring you more money to go toward the retainer." She leaned in closer. "I want him to give you as much money as possible so that you can be extra-motivated to give my daughter your best work."

In a strange way Mrs. Londers reminded Yarni of her own mother. Though they shared no resemblance at all, they both loved their daughters immensely. "What I do is not about the money. Understand, I want to be paid," she said with a slight smile, "but when I take on a case I'm either all in or I don't take it. So please don't worry, Mrs. Londers, I will do my best on Tangaleena's case," Yarni assured her as she looked into the eyes of a woman who wore much worry, hurt and pain across her face.

"Thank you, dear. I believe you will, but I want you to get your money first thing."

"If you insist." Yarni changed the subject. "Do you know if your daughter has any priors?" Normally, Yarni would have this information at hand, but with all the drama going on, time had gotten away from her.

Mrs. Londers took a deep breath and nodded. "I'm afraid so. She has quite a few, but nothing in at least four years. She used to fight a lot." Her mother rolled her eyes. "She's been known to pull out a can of whip ass at the drop of a dime. But over the past four years, since she's had her daughter, she hasn't gotten in any trouble. Not a drop. "

"Okay, so she's a mother?" Yarni knew that would help in showing stability and could be a good factor in why this woman deserved bond.

"Yes," she smiled, "and that little girl means the world to her."

"I bet she does. Well, let's go in there and try to get the two back together, where they belong."

"God bless you, Mrs. Taylor."

Yarni gave Mrs. Londers a comforting pat on the shoulder, then headed for the courtroom.

Inside, Yarni quietly sat on the hard mahogany wooden slabs most courthouses used for seating.

She wasn't yet concerned about the actual charges—assault and possession of a gun after being convicted of a felony. But she was slightly worried about Tangaleena's priors becoming the focal point of this bond hearing and how that might affect the outcome.

Yarni grimaced at the fact that Judge Fairchild was presiding on the bench. Sometimes this particular judge's decisions were not always as fair as her name may lead one to believe. But over the last few years, she and Yarni had developed a somewhat decent working rapport. After watching the judge rule in more than a hundred cases, Yarni was familiar with her tactics. She felt even better after seeing that Judge Fairchild was in a decent mood.

"Who do we have next?" she asked her court clerk, who had a head of white hair and a long pointed nose holding a pair of huge glasses.

"Tangaleena Londers versus the State of Virginia," the clerk announced. "She's charged with assault and possession of a firearm." Just as the clerk finished speaking, Yarni took her place at the defense table, waiting for her client to be brought into the courtroom. The deputy ushered the inmate from the back, wearing the traditional city jail uniform: brown khaki scrubs and orange slip-on canvas deck shoes. Yarni smiled at Tangaleena, laying eyes on her for the first time. She was a pretty, well-groomed girl. Even in a jail uniform she looked good. Her skin was smooth and had a healthy glow to it. She had been in jail since Monday and it was now Thursday. There was no indication at all that she had been in a fight, at least not on the losing end.

Yarni turned around to look at Mrs. Londers before the proceedings began. She wanted to give her a reassuring look, but she was distracted by the guy who had taken a seat beside the woman. He looked to be in his early forties, average height, rail thin, with peanut butter–colored skin.

A chill ran down Yarni's spine. *How do I know him? A past client?* she thought. *Do I know him through Des?* His head was turned as he said something to Mrs. Londers. Then he turned to face the front, and his round pop eyes met Yarni's, causing her to feel like she was in a scene from throw-back boxing, when a young and new Mike Tyson hit Michael Spinks with the legendary right hook.

There wasn't a chance in hell that she'd ever forget that beetle-bug face. It had definitely been a long time ago, well over a decade, almost two, but she remembered it like it was yesterday. Her feet were like cement blocks planted there on the courtroom floor. She couldn't move, and before she knew it, her mind had flashed back to the way their paths had crossed long ago. And though it had been over seventeen years ago, she remembered it like it was just yesterday.

$ $ $

It was 2:30 in the morning when Yarni and her girlfriend, Vanessa, walked out of the front door of Ivory's Uptown Lounge with an attitude.

"That shit was so wack," Yarni complained.

"You ain't never lied," Vanessa echoed her displeasure. "That shit was a waste of my makeup and time."

The only thing Yarni and Vanessa really had in common was going out to the clubs. If Yarni needed a shoulder to cry on or even someone to go shopping with, Vanessa wasn't the one she called. The twosome knew a lot of the same people and both could do the damn thing when it came to dressing. Partying and clubbing while looking fabulous was in their blood, so they often went out together.

"Let's not forget this outfit." Yarni was wearing a dress from LaVogue that had set her back at least four hundred bills. By the way she wore it, though, it looked like it could have cost four grand.

Vanessa cut her eyes, barely able to disguise her envy. "I know those shoes gotta hurt your feet."

Yarni looked down at her feet, on which she'd donned three-inch heels with blinged-out straps. "Fashion sometimes comes with a little pain," she said.

"Well, mine don't hurt and I didn't pay half of what you paid."

"Don't hate, congratulate," Yarni wanted to remind Vanessa, but instead she changed the subject. "You want me to walk with you to your car, and then you give me a ride back to mine?" *Better safe than sorry,* Yarni thought to herself.

"Naw, I'm okay. I'm parked right up the street." Vanessa pointed to her car.

That was one of the reasons Yarni didn't kick it with her outside of clubbing. Vanessa never thought about anyone but herself, but Yarni shrugged it off. "Well, a'ight. I'm parked in the other direction." Yarni still gave her friend a hug, and as she walked off she said, "Call me when you get home."

"Who said I was going straight home?" Vanessa giggled. "I might stop and put something in my stomach, like some hot fries . . . or a long, hard, thick dick."

"That shit would be funny if I didn't know you were dead-ass serious," Yarni shot back, knowing Vanessa's M.O. It was senseless trying to talk Vanessa out of something once she put her mind to it, so Yarni did the next best thing. "Just be careful . . . and make sure you make your donor carry an umbrella and wear a raincoat," she advised over her shoulder.

"I don't leave home without 'em. You must have forgotten . . . I graduated from my sex education class magnum cum laude."

This bitch is silly, Yarni thought to herself, trying not to burst into laughter. "Well, I'll call you later. Don't do anything you'll regret in the morning."

"I don't do regrets," Vanessa retorted. "They get in the way of the fun."

Yarni was thinking about some of the crazy antics Vanessa had pulled in the past as she turned the corner at Grace Street. It was packed with cars, but as far as people, it was a ghost town. Everyone must have still been getting their groove on inside the various bars and clubs, getting liquored up and/or trying to find somebody to go home with.

With her car a block ahead, Yarni fumbled in her purse searching for her keys, to have them on standby. Preoccupied, she never heard the blue Caravan creep up from behind until it was almost too late. The side door slid open and a young man clad in dark jeans and a black T-shirt jumped out.

"Lookie at what I done stumbled upon," he sang as he pulled up his sagging pants to his waist with an up-to-no-good mischievous grin plastered on his face. "It must be one of our lucky days."

Totally caught off guard, alone and vulnerable, Yarni could

barely keep up with all the wild thoughts that started running through her head.

The young hoodlum had pockmarked skin and the arrogant swagger of a playground bully. She wanted to say something that would, maybe, persuade him to second-guess his plans, but she was unable to trust her own voice from giving away her secret: she was afraid for her life.

A dark minivan filled with God only knew how many people on a back street with a harmless young girl as their prey. Nothing good usually came from these types of situations. Rape? Robbery? Kidnapping? Or worse, murder? Her mind raced back to the past and she thought to herself, *Not again. History could not and was not going to repeat.*

She had gotten snatched and held for ransom almost a year ago to the day. For the most part the ambitious thugs didn't mean her any harm. They were hungry and saw her as a quick come-up. She was to be nothing more than a meal ticket, to get them what made the world go around: money. But when her then big-time, dope-dealing boyfriend, Bengee, got the ransom call, he laughed and hung up, but not before informing the kidnappers that it was cheaper for them to keep her because he wasn't coming off one copper penny. And he never paid the ransom they were requesting. It was one of the scariest things Yarni had ever had happen to her. If it weren't for the hundred thousand dollars her mother and Uncle Stanka somehow came up with—not to mention her not panicking, keeping her composure and thinking on her feet—she was sure the kidnappers would have raped and killed her.

Now Yarni feared a repeat episode, knowing that most people are not lucky enough to be spared twice in a row. She took a deep breath as adrenaline overtook her body. The thug in the baggy pants inched closer, and whatever this dude had on his mind, Yarni knew she wanted no part of it. Scared or not, she was prepared to fight until there wasn't a breath left in her body.

Inside her purse, she wrapped her hand around the .380 small caliber pistol her uncle Stanka had given to her after she had been kidnapped. She deliberately had some loose stitching in the lining of one of the pockets to hide the gun. That way when club security searched the contents of her purse with their flashlights, it would go undetected. So thanks to Yarni's weapon of choice, this clown in front of her wouldn't be the only one with a bag full of surprises tonight. Yarni contemplated her next move, and it was so unpredictable that nobody, not even Yarni, had expected it.

Without warning a brazen sound erupted. Pop! Pop! Yarni let off two shots straight through her pocketbook. It stunned the van passengers, causing an "Oh Shit" to come from one.

The shots rang out so fast, the thug was stunned for a brief moment. He'd frozen in mid-step, but only for a second. Once he saw the shot was fired into the ground and not him, he regrouped, sizing her up as Yarni met his eyes. She saw a smirk on his face as if this was all some big joke. But this wasn't a game that Yarni was playing. This was her life and she planned to live it past the twenty years she'd already experienced on Earth.

"Bug, come on," the driver of the van hollered. "Let it go, Bug. Let's bounce." But Bug ignored him.

"Fuck dat," the young thug stated. "I got this. Shit is bubble gum! I ain't never in my life been shook up by no bitch, with or without a gun." He and Yarni were having a Mexican standoff with their eyes.

This was the first time that Yarni had ever fired a gun. When her uncle gave it to her he said to never pull it out unless you are going to use it. And if she waited too long after pulling it, she may lose her opportunity. Bug, inching closer, looked to be bold enough to try to take the gun away from her, which wasn't an option for her, not at this moment or in this situation. Nerves caused her head to spin and hand to shake a little. But that didn't stop her from doing what she had to do.

The next shot Yarni fired was another warning shot into the ground. She hoped it would persuade him to put some pep in his step in the opposite direction from where she was going. Instead of scaring him off, it did the exact opposite, increasing his confidence. He equated the wasted bullet in the ground with weakness, not strength, and moved in on her.

"You mine, bitch," he said through gritted teeth, letting go of the baggy pants he'd had a death grip on in order to charge at Yarni. "Bitches should never play with grown men." He yelled when he lurched toward her.

Wrong move. Yarni squeezed off another shot. This time the bullet slammed into Bug's leg. Finally realizing he'd messed with the wrong one, the wounded young thug tried to turn and run from the trouble he had started. He was too slow, though. He caught another one slam dab in his rear end. "Shit!" he cried out. His ass was on fire. "Crazy bitch!" He tried to make his way back to the van. Whatever had been on his mind was now on his ass, as he hobbled in pain.

Still afraid that his friends may get out of the van and come to their comrade's rescue with machine guns or something, Yarni made out like one of Charlie's Angels and quickly pointed her weapon at the vehicle. She was feeling scared and invincible at the same time. "Hey, you motherfuckers! It ain't like you thought it would be, is it? Now get the fuck on." She simultaneously let a couple more shots off on in the direction of the van as she screamed at them. It was becoming easier by the second to pull the trigger on these fools.

Pedal to the metal, the driver of the van mashed out. He skidded off, burning up rubber trying to get the hell out of Dodge, leaving Bug to fend for himself.

"Fuck you going?" Bug screamed in frustration and disgust. To make matters worse, his pants, as baggy as they were, dropped to the ground. He hopped off after the van with his jeans around his ankles, watching the taillights of the getaway car signaling to turn. He was hoping they would wait on him around the corner. With his naked rear end exposed, he watched the taillights vanish and realized he was assed out in more ways than one.

6

Back to Reality . . .
in the Courtroom

"Counselor Pitman-Taylor, are you the attorney for this case?"
Judge Fairchild repeated.

The sound of the judge's voice instantly brought Yarni's
thoughts back to the courtroom. "Yes, Your Honor, I'll be repre-
senting Ms. Londers." For the moment, Yarni put aside the
memory of the past situation and the man, Bug, sitting in the
back of the courtroom. The man who would have done only
God knows what if she hadn't pulled the trigger. The man she
had almost forgotten about until he waltzed into the courtroom.
She peered into his eyes one more time, searching for any sign of
recollection, and saw nothing but fear and urgency for his girlfriend.

Yarni acknowledged her client, who looked like a woman

eager to be restored to the rightful place in the free world, and Tangaleena smiled at Yarni in return.

Prosecutor Lawrence Little III stood to his full height of 5'7", straightened his yellow tie, then cleared his throat before speaking. "The state recommends that the defendant be remanded into the state's custody without bond, Your Honor."

Underneath her breath, Yarni quipped, "I bet the state does."

Yarni and this particular prosecuting attorney had never gotten along and had been through more than their share of heated litigation battles. Yarni was well aware that Little hated her guts. Aside from him being a male chauvinist, he felt like she wasn't worthy of having a law degree. Let Little tell it—and he did every chance he got—he was sure that Des was still involved in some type of criminal activity. How else could a black man that wasn't an entertainer or professional athlete afford to buy a Bentley? Where would he get money to start up an exotic car dealership the moment he was released from prison? And birds of a feather flocked together, as far as Little was concerned. Which made Mrs. Yarnise Taylor guilty by association. He lived for the day when he could prove his theories and convict Des. That would truly make his dick hard. But he wouldn't climax until he found a way to have Yarni disbarred.

Yarni welcomed the opportunity to once again defeat Little but she was starting to have second thoughts about the case. If the guy she knew as Bug was her client's boyfriend, and he remembered that she had shot him, things could get complicated. Surely it was a conflict of interest that could come back to bite her later, she thought. She decided she'd shoot for the bond, spanking the prosecutor, then dismiss herself from the case.

"Your Honor, my client has lived in the Richmond area her entire life. She is the sole support for her four-year-old daughter and has no reason, nor any desire, to skip her obligation of attending trial. In fact," Yarni added, "she relishes the opportunity to clear her name of these undeserving charges." Then she turned to and peered over at her courtroom nemesis with professional courtesy. To no one's surprise, Prosecutor Little wasn't done yet.

"Ms. Londers," Little started again, "is a career criminal who was once connected to the infamous Waltz-Londers Gang that terrorized the south side of Richmond just a few years back. These people were known for using violence and intimidation, as casually as you and I put our shoes and socks on in the morning."

"This is ridiculous, Judge." Yarni folded her arms as she stood, when Little had finished. "The trial of the Waltz-Londers Gang, as they were labeled by the media, took place nearly twenty years ago. That would have made my client about five or six years old. Clearly Prosecutor Little is exaggerating, or delusional, or both. Her connection, as Mr. Little put it, is nonexistent. Because of my client's last name, Mr. Little has essentially handcuffed her to the ghost of Richmond's past in an attempt to paint a picture that just doesn't exist." Yarni had everyone's attention. "Moreover—"

The judge interrupted. "I've heard enough, Counselors." She looked over Tangaleena's rap sheet. "Ms. Londers, I see you've got some anger issues—however, I think we may be able to agree on an equitable outcome based on what I've heard. How about I set a bond at fifty thousand dollars, and—"

"With all due respect, Judge Fairchild," Yarni voiced her opinion, "fifty thousand may be a bit excessive given the circumstances."

"Your client is a," Little interrupted, speaking over Yarni, "your client is no lady. She's a menace to society," Little blurted out.

"The only menace here is you," Yarni shot back.

Judge Fairchild gave a piercing stare to Little, and Yarni felt the pendulum sway her way. "Don't press your luck, Counselor Pitman-Taylor—or you, Counselor Little. This isn't a suggestion, it is my ruling." She removed her glasses as if to finalize her point. "Bail is set at thirty thousand, and Ms. Londers, you must stay out of trouble. One hit, one punch, one uppercut, one jaywalking, and your bond will be revoked. Do you understand?"

Tangaleena nodded.

Yarni smiled. "Thank you very much, Your Honor." The interruption was well worth getting the judge to drop 20k off her own original decision.

As the bailiff was placing the handcuffs back on Tangaleena's wrists, Yarni leaned in and softly asked her client if she thought she would be able to raise the money for the bond.

"Yes, I think so. Thank you so much," Tangaleena responded with a sigh of relief, visibly proud that this woman was her attorney.

"No problem, but I'm going to need you to come by my office when you get out of here." The deputy was in a hurry to haul Tangaleena back to the holding cell, so Yarni quickly let the words roll off her tongue as she put a business card in the shirt pocket of her client's jail uniform.

Tangaleena nodded. "I'll be there as soon as I break outta here." The bailiff took her to the back. Her family would only have to come up with three thousand dollars, ten percent of the thirty thousand to get her out. Tangaleena looked at her mother, who was now standing at the first pew. "Baby, Dougie got a bondman on standby, so you should be out in a little while. Okay?" Mrs. Londers spoke to her daughter.

Tangaleena nodded as the deputy led her off.

Yarni looked toward the rear of the courtroom for the man whose ass she had busted a cap in back in the day. He was nowhere to be found, though. It was as if he'd disappeared into thin air.

7

Dragon Balls

The brownstone that housed the law firm of Pitman-Taylor had been restored beyond its original brilliance and sat regally in the heart of the historic and legendary Jackson Ward. It was in this same neighborhood where the first black female banker, Maggie Walker, lived, and the famous tap dancer Bill "Bojangles" Robinson and his friends once partied. Ironically, at one time it was also the home of Richmond's most infamous housing projects.

Yarni loved the area with all its rich African American history. There was never a dull moment in Jackson Ward, with its diverse culture comprised of people from all walks of life and social settings. There were the old and new residents, the black and the white, the rich and the poor. The neighborhood was a character in itself and seemed to keep Yarni grounded somehow. Her office was meticulously furnished, although on some days, like today, the aesthetics would be disturbed by the stacks of folders thrown haphazardly across her French-style desk. Let her tell it, some of her best strategies came from the energy of the clutter that surrounded her.

Since returning from court, she had closed herself off in her office, fully focused on work, not wanting to deal with any of the madness that was going on in her personal life. She had been going over the same case for more than two hours when Layla, her assistant and office paralegal, buzzed.

"There's a Ms. Tangaleena Londers here to see you, but she doesn't have an appointment. She said you told her to come by once she got out of the slammer."

Layla always delivered messages exactly the way she received them.

"They sure didn't waste any time bailing her out," Yarni said. "Ask her how about we schedule her for tomorrow. This appeal I'm working on is kicking my butt."

"That's why I'm sending her in—you need to break up some of the monotony." And the phone went dead.

Layla was good at her job but she could be a bit pushy sometimes.

Moments later there was a slight tap on the door and Yarni said, "Come in." When it opened, she was impressed by how well Tangaleena looked out of the jail uniform.

A young lady with a bronze complexion, long auburn hair extensions that had been straightened out and a thin build, with some Marc Jacobs frames covering her eyes, walked into the office.

Yarni stood to shake her hand. "How are you, Ms. Londers?" Yarni smiled, then pointed to a chair. "Have a seat." She then looked to her assistant. "Thank you, Layla," signaling that it was okay for her to get back to work.

Tangaleena sat in the yellow leather chair. She removed her sunglasses and placed them in her Marc Jacobs bag. "First, let me say that I was very pleased with you today in court."

"I'm glad it was to your satisfaction. Thank you very much." But Yarni didn't hesitate to get down to business. "So what exactly happened?" The fact that she'd planned to remove herself from the case was the last thing on Yarni's mind. Tangaleena was shifting in the chair, which showed that she was a little uncomfortable. Yarni looked into her client's eyes. "And I'd like to remind you that whatever you say here can't and *won't* be held against you, because of attorney/client privilege."

"Well, since you put it like that." Tangaleena looked down and was playing with her hands, but becoming a little more comfortable. "It's sort of a long story." She sighed. "I hope you have a minute."

"I do," Yarni told her, at this point glad that she had taken the break from the appeal she was working on. There was something about Tangaleena that she liked.

Leaning forward in the leather chair on the opposite side of the desk, the young woman still appeared nervous. Maybe it was more fear than nerves; the two emotions shared the same DNA. Tangaleena took a deep breath. "If I don't beat this case, my life might as well be over," she surmised.

"Why do you say that? The charges you have against you are serious but it's not that bad."

"Yeah, but things are really complicated. There's more here than what's seen on the surface."

"Then help me see what you see." Yarni gave Tangaleena her undivided attention.

"Well, I adopted a beautiful little girl three years ago. At the time she was one year old. Her mother was a straight crackhead." She shook her head. "Just a no-good junkie."

A slight smile spread across Yarni's lips. Ignoring the last comment, she said, "Oh, how sweet. My sister did the same thing, she adopted a child too." She let the girl continue telling her story.

"Well, maybe you can understand my plight, then." She made eye contact with Yarni. "The baby's father is my first cousin, we call 'im Shortee. He was sentenced to thirty years in prison for robbery the day Spumante was born. Spumante is the little girl."

Yarni wanted to shake her head at the poor child's name, but stayed focused on the topic at hand instead.

But Tangaleena must have read Yarni's mind. "Yeah, I know," she said. "The name, right? Her momma thought she was giving her a French name."

Yarni remained silent. She'd learned over the years of being an attorney that the less she intervened, the more people tended to talk.

"Make no mistake about it; both of the parents are a hot ass mess. Matter of fact, the best thing that Shortee could have ever done in his miserable life was to give his sperm to create that child. But this ain't about him; this here is about her crackhead carrier, Chiquita. Three days after delivering Monte, that's what I call her, she figured out that she had no intention of raising a baby. So she brought Monte to my eighty-five-year-old grand-mother's house, supposedly went to the bathroom, and slipped out through the back door. The next time any of us heard from her, she showed up trying to sell us some baby clothes that she had boosted from a discount store. Am I moving too fast?" she stopped to ask Yarni, who was taking notes.

"You are not moving fast enough" is what Yarni wanted to say, but she simply responded, "Not at all."

"You know I'm about to tell you the whole truth, and nothing but the truth, so help me God. You gotta believe this is what happened."

"I'm all ears."

"I'm going to give it to you, exactly the way it went down."

Yarni turned to a clean page on her legal pad, kicked back, turned her listening ear on high, and took a ride down memory lane with her client.

"After not hearing from Chiquita for nearly four years, I got a call from Shortee," Tangaleena started, relaying the conversation and that day's events verbatim.

$ $ $

"Whadit do, cuzo?"

"Nothing much. Spumante watching TV and I'm trying to straighten up around here."

"How baby girl doing?"

"She's doing good, just growing big."

"Yo, let me make this shit real quick, 'cause they be tripping 'bout the phone 'round here."

"A'ight then, don't worry about the small talk. What's good? What you need?" Tangaleena figured that Shortee either needed something or had some kind of prison gossip to pass on.

"You heard about Chiquita just coming home from doing dem ten months dem peeps gave her, right?"

"I heard she was out, but you know you can't believe half of what you hear."

Shortee chuckled. "The word on the street is since she been out, she's been spending a lot of energy trying to make up for lost time."

"I'm not shocked."

"How come you not shocked?" Shortee asked.

"I mean really, are you? Come on now—fuck milk, ten months clean in the county does the body good," she joked, but was dead serious. "Because you know firsthand one thing about being locked down, you get plenty of rest and three meals a day."

"Well, word is that after two hours of her being home, she had tricks throwing money. She always did know how to treat a dick. That girl is a beast."

"Shortee," Tangaleena interrupted. "I don't want to hear all that."

"I know, forgive me. A nigga in the pen gotta have some good thoughts from the streets. But anyways, let me get back to this worthless bitch. Well, within two weeks she was back getting high and I heard she's been smoking—heroin mixed with cooked coke. Some folks call it dragon balls. When you smoke that shit you feel as if there's nothing you can't do."

"So?" Tangaleena tried to get Shortee to the point. He could be really long-winded sometimes.

"I just want to give you a heads-up," Shortee warned. "Just so you know what the word is on the street."

After hanging up with her cousin, Tangaleena wondered why he had even called her with that senseless bullshit. Did he still love Chiquita? Whatever the reason was, she really didn't connect the dots or care. She redirected her attention to the housework, washing dishes while Spumante sat on the couch drinking hot chocolate and watching *Shrek* for the hundredth time. The doorbell rang and Spumante came running into the kitchen. "Who's at the door, Mommy?"

"I don't know, baby, let's go see," she said as she wiped her hands on a towel.

She walked to the door and looked out the window. She saw a woman who resembled Chiquita too much not to be her. She was wearing a pair of supertight stretch jeans, black sneakers and a black leather coat.

It was definitely Chiquita, Tangaleena concluded, but what the fuck could she want? She didn't look too bad; maybe Shortee was wrong about the drugs. Reluctantly and naively, Tangaleena undid the lock and opened the door. "May I help you?" she asked with less enthusiasm than she would've exuded for a vacuum cleaner salesman.

"Dang, gurl, you ain't gotta act like that." Chiquita and Tangaleena never really got along. Chiquita hadn't liked the fact that Tangaleena was Shortee's favorite cousin and they were close.

"What are you doing on my steps?" Tangaleena asked.

Spumante was on her knees on the sofa, peeking over with her round inquisitive eyes. She wanted to know who it was at the door. "Who is dat, Mommy?"

"Nobody, baby," Tangaleena said, regretting that she had even opened the door for the woman. "Just keep watching the DVDs."

"Is that Spumante I hear?" Chiquita said with a glassy look in her eyes. Before Tangaleena realized it, the crack-addicted woman had stepped into the apartment uninvited. "Oh my *God*, you done got so big," she said once she saw the baby she'd abandoned three years ago. When she tried to get closer, Spumante ran and hid behind Tangaleena, the only mother she ever knew.

"How do dat lady know who I am, Mommy? I don't know who she is." Spumante shook her head from side to side and said, "I don't talk to strangers, right, Mommy?"

"That's right, that's my smart little angel."

Chiquita sucked her teeth. "Stop filling that girl's head up with that nonsense, Tang. You know I ain't no motherfucking stranger to her or to you. So gon ahead wit dat shit."

"Bitch, the mailman is less of a stranger than yo' missing-in-action ass," is what Tangaleena had wanted to say, just before popping Chiquita's selfish ass upside the head with a toaster or something. She didn't, though. She didn't want to create any more of a scene in front of Spumante.

Chiquita's eyes tracked Spumante hiding behind Tangaleena's leg. "I'm your moth—"

"Friend." Tangaleena's voice was louder and she spoke over top of Chiquita, saying "Your mother's friend."

"Yep. Me and your mother go back like jelly shoes," Chiquita played along. Tangaleena was grateful for that.

Spumante looked confused. "Mommy, you had shoes made of jelly?" She laughed with a big adorable smile.

"I'll tell you about 'em later, baby. That was a long, long time ago," Tangaleena told her daughter. She then turned her attention back to Chiquita. "What're you doing here anyway?"

"Exactly what it looks like—I'm visiting an old friend and seeing my baby girl."

This bitch was definitely pushing her luck. "We're kind of busy right now. You should've called first, girl. How about if you drop through some other time?" Hindsight is twenty/twenty, and she now knew that opening the door for this heifer had been the wrong move. She'd naively put her head in the lion's mouth, now she was trying to carefully ease it back out without cutting herself on its teeth. But she could now see clearly that Chiquita was high as the rising price of gas. When she looked at her, she realized that more and more the bitch started to resemble the devil's half sister.

"I ain't trying to hear none of that shit you talking, you thieving-ass bitch. Acting all high and mighty like you really my daughter's mother. Got her calling you mommy and shit. You ain't none of her momma." Before Tangaleena could react, Chiquita whipped out a big butcher's knife. "How 'bout I take Spumante with me and call you when I'm ready to bring her back? Better yet, when I'm ready for yo' stuck-up ass to see her?" And Chiquita reached for Spumante's arm.

Spumante cried out to Tangaleena, "Mommy!" and tried to pull away.

This had to be a bad dream, Tangaleena thought. Was there really a knife-wielding crackhead in her house trying to take her daughter?

Instinctively, Tangaleena reached to pull Spumante away from this crazy woman. Chiquita made an arching sweep of her hand while holding the blade, drawing blood from Tangaleena's arm. With the strength of a mother grizzly trying to protect her cub, Tangaleena disregarded her own safety and jumped on Chiquita. The knife bit her a few more times before they both went to the floor, tussling. It was on.

The effect of the narcotics made Chiquita fight like a madwoman. Her grip was viselike, too strong for Tangaleena. When Chiquita clamped her hands around Tangaleena's neck, Tangaleena knew it wouldn't be long before she passed out if she didn't do something fast.

For a split second all she envisioned was herself passed out and Chiquita going out the door with Spumante in tow. In her head, she silently repeated the words *God help me!* God must not have been too busy because that's when she caught sight of her brass duck ornament. It was just a foot or so away. Thank God it was close enough for her to reach. Tangaleena got her hands on the solid ornament and with all her might she slammed that sucker against Chiquita's temple. Chiquita immediately let go of Tangaleena's neck, clutching for the side of her head where she'd been hit. Blood was squirting out her clinched fingers.

That was all the time Tangaleena needed to jump up. Once she was on her feet, she ran in the kitchen and got the gun that Bug kept in the top cabinet.

"Play time is over, you crazy bitch. Get the fuck out of my house." Tangaleena had the gun in one hand and her cell in the other dialing 911. Spumante had run for cover but she was crying, calling for her mommy. That's the part that broke Tangaleena's heart. Ironically, the same time the police pulled up, so did her boyfriend, Bug.

$ $ $

When Tangaleena mentioned Bug's name, that's what snapped Yarni back to reality in her office and caused her to remember why she had thought about dropping the case before she had even gotten started.

"Sounds like you were lucky to not have gotten hurt," Yarni said, knowing good and well that there was no way she could turn Tangaleena away even though she was still unsure of whether Bug remembered her or if he held a grudge for her giving it to him in the butt.

"When the police got to my house," Tangaleena continued her story, "they had the nerve to charge me for being in possession of a gun, and assault. And that bitch tried to kill me and take my little girl. They locked us both up. It's still hard for me to believe that shit." Tangaleena said.

"I should be able to get the charge dropped to a misdemeanor," Yarni said, now with a clearer understanding of what had happened. "The sentence will only be a slap on the wrist at best."

"Yeah, but it's not quite that simple. I got ten years suspended sentence over my head when I was eighteen for beating this other chick's ass who cussed out my momma. See, don't fuck with my family. I don't play that. But if I get found guilty of anything," she shook her head, "they gonna slap me with a probation violation and then send me to the penitentiary. That can't happen."

Just then, Layla buzzed in. "Mrs. Taylor, Des called and said your mother-in-law will be at your house within the hour and that he'd meet you at home. You need to leave ASAP."

"Thank you, Layla. I'm wrapping up this meeting now," Yarni said.

"Well, I know I have occupied a lot of your day, and I thank you," Tangaleena said in a humble tone. "I really feel that my boyfriend's cousin was right."

"Your boyfriend's cousin?" Yarni questioned.

"Yes, he was the one who recommended you and I'm glad he did."

"What's his name so I can thank him?" she asked.

"I don't know, but I will ask Bug," she said. "Well, I'll check in a week or so to see if there is anything you need me to do on my end to prepare. But can you think of anything now?"

"Besides keep your jabs to yourself?"

Tangaleena laughed as she headed for the door. "Oh, you really don't have to worry about that."

"Let's definitely chat within the next two weeks, and thanks for coming by."

Tangaleena exited the office, and Yarni began to gather her things to head home to meet her eighteen-year-old stepdaughter whom she'd known nothing about until less than twenty-four hours ago.

Once she hit the chirp to unlock her car, she noticed that Tangaleena had been outside waiting. "Do you need a ride?" Yarni asked.

"No, but thanks. My boyfriend should be pulling up any second."

"Well, I'd feel better if you would wait inside," Yarni suggested.

Just as she said that, a Q45 pulled up. Tangaleena's face lit up. "Here he is." It was her ride.

"Okay, great."

Yarni went to grab the door on her car when the window of the Infiniti came down. "Yo, Mrs. Taylor, 'preciate you getting my girl out," Bug said, still with no indication that he had any recollection of Yarni whatsoever.

"Not a problem at all," Yarni flashed a fake smile.

She got in her car and pulled out from her parking space en route for home. She turned an old-school reggae CD up and tried to put her mind on cruise control because she had a feeling that between her new client and her stepdaughter, her life was about to get even more hectic than it already was.

8

Momma's Baby; Daddy's Maybe

"Yeah, we almost at your house now. How long before you get there?"

Desember ear-hustled as Joyce drove with both hands on the steering wheel of her Mercedes-Benz at ten and two as she spoke on the phone through her Bluetooth.

"Ten minutes?"

From the passenger seat, Desember watched Joyce glance at the built-in navigation screen. It read twenty-three minutes until arrival at destination.

"Good," Joyce said, "you should beat us there. We about twenty-five minutes away. Did Yarni fix anything to eat?"

Judging by the expression on Joyce's face, she must not have gotten the right answer. "What ya mean why we didn't stop? Who said we didn't stop?" She was twisting her neck now. "But what the hell does that got to do with anything? I asked you did your wife cook anything at your house." She listened for a brief second before responding, "Just make sure your smart ass be home when we get there."

And that was the end of the call.

Joyce took her eyes off the road for a split second, peeking at her granddaughter. "That was your daddy talking shit. That joker always got some slick shit to say. Make me want to smack the hell out of him."

Desember went along with the flow. All her life, all she ever wanted to know was the identity of her real daddy. Eighteen years was a long time . . . a long time not to know who her father was.

When Desember was three years old the man she believed to be her daddy decided he wasn't too sure about paternity. A DNA test made what he suspected a reality. It played out like a Maury Povich show: "You are not the father!"

"What does he look like?" Desember asked.

"Who . . . Des?" Joyce asked, taking another quick peek at the navigation screen. "He looks a whole lot like you," she said. "Except you're a lot prettier than he is."

As far as Desember was concerned, the jury was still out on her grandmother Joyce. Just a minute ago she was on the phone cussing Desember's could-be father out in one breath. Now here she was in the next breath telling Desember how pretty she was—Joyce wasn't exactly what she had imagined a nanna to be.

The only grandmother that Desember had ever known was Lizabell, her mother's mother. Lizabell and Joyce were as different as water and wine. Lizabell was soft-spoken, loved to bake, was religious and had never uttered a cuss word in her life. She also never stood up for herself or raised her voice to anyone. And she raised her daughter, Angie, to be the same way. Joyce was nothing like either of them. But that suited Desember just fine, because neither was she.

Desember looked over at Joyce, giving her a discreet once-over. *Wasn't grannies suppose to wear muumuus?* Desember asked herself, observing how Joyce was dressed to the nines in a jean suit and blinged-out flats. Her hair was fried, dyed, and laid to the side.

Desember's vision of a granny was hardly the lady who had picked her up three hours ago. Though Joyce had to be pushing at least seventy, she looked damn good for her age. If it was true that black don't crack, Joyce was a living testament. Her skin was smooth as the face of a porcelain doll. She cursed like a drunken sailor when and to whom she felt like. The woman was a pistol and Desember was sure she packed one too. It was hard to imagine anyone trying to run over her.

If Des proved to be her daddy, and the jury was still out on that, maybe she had gotten her spunkiness and heart from Grandmother Joyce. After all, Desember's mouth had gotten her in and out of trouble more times than she cared to count or remember.

Joyce broke the silence. "What's on your mind, young lady?"

"I was just thinking." Desember looked out the window, watching the white lines blur by on the black pavement on the other side of the window.

"About what?" Joyce asked. "You can share with me if you want. I'm a good listener and I can keep a secret." Joyce gave her an infectious smile.

"You ain't lying about the secret." Then Desember sighed and answered Joyce's initial question. "About everything."

"Well, young lady, everything can be overwhelming for anybody to try to carry around. Maybe you should try lightening your load," Joyce advised.

"I'm not sure I did the right thing by leaving North Carolina," she admitted. "I mean, I'm kinda happy to finally meet my real dad. But . . ." Desember paused.

Joyce urged her to go on. "But what, baby?"

Desember sighed again. "I'm going to keep it real with you. My boyfriend, Fame, got shot just three days ago. I was in the car with him and for the most part I don't think I should be allowed to feel happy while he feels nothing but pain."

"Why would someone shoot your boyfriend?" Joyce kept her eyes on the road as Desember thought about the question. "Is he a bad person . . . or the victim of a bad person?"

Desember thought about the questions. Fame had damn near robbed every big-name drug dealer in North Carolina and was good at it. She smiled to herself thinking about the time Fame's partner backed out on the score they'd planned on a dope boy that owned a strip club. "One monkey don't stop no show," she'd said to him, "take me with you." And he did.

Fame dressed up like a chick, even got hit on by a couple of dudes, but with Desember's help, took care of the business. They got over two hundred thousand in cash before making their way out the back exit, leaving the guy and his bodyguard tied up and pissed off. Better to be pissed off than pissed on.

"Well, baby?" Joyce said, interrupting Desember's thoughts.

"To be honest," she said truthfully, "probably a little bit of both. He's a good person, but sometimes does bad things. Does that make any sense?"

"All the sense in the world, baby."

The answer put a slight smile on Desember's face as she looked out the window up at the gray sky. She had mixed feelings about going to live with her supposed father and his wife. Regardless of the danger involved, she didn't want to leave Fame, her first love, fighting for his life, even if people were looking to kill her. She didn't care because Fame was her world and being with him fulfilled her in ways she was unable to explain.

But from his hospital bed in the ICU, Fame insisted that she leave town until he was better and could protect her. She followed his wishes, and that was the only reason she went along with her mother's plan to move her in with her father.

The only good thing that may have come out of this was the possibility of having the one dream granted that she ever really had—to meet her real father. She just hoped Angie was telling the truth and this wasn't some bullshit concoction to get her out of town. After all, it wouldn't be the first time her mother had plugged a man into her life playing daddy, and once the paternity test came in, none of them were who she claimed them to be. But this time, maybe just this one time, it might be true.

After a while, Joyce drove into a long, circular driveway and stopped in front of a huge home. Desember could not believe her eyes. The house looked like paradise. Though she knew that she shouldn't judge a book by its cover, most of the time it was all she could judge it by. Her mother had always provided a nice place for them to live, but never anything as lavish as the house she sat in front of now.

Even in the winter, there were at least two acres of some of the greenest grass Desember had ever seen. It surrounded a house that had to be at least ten thousand square feet of stunning architecture. If the exterior was this incredible, she couldn't even imagine what the inside looked like.

"Finally," Joyce said, relief evident in her voice. "We're here. That ride kicked my butt. And now I gots to pee."

Desember was still staring at the house.

"It's nice, isn't it? Yarni, your daddy's wife, helped with most of the design. The builders had to have her approval on every little thing, from the marble and hardwood floors to the custom-shingled roof. Drove those poor damn workers crazy."

During the ride in, Desember had asked Joyce several questions about Des. And Joyce seemed to love talking about her son and other granddaughter, Desi. But this was the first time that Desember inquired about Des's wife. "Do you like her? My father's wife, is she pretty cool people?"

"Well, in the past her and I didn't and still don't always see eye to eye, but for the most part, she's a good person. High maintenance. Likes nice shit, you know."

"You look like you do too, Ms. Joyce," Desember said, basing the comment on her could-be grandmother's Louis Vuitton bag, designer outfit and top-of-the-line Mercedes-Benz.

Joyce blushed. "Oh hell yeah. But she's a lawyer with a real good heart. Over the years we had our ups and downs. I mean we battled." Joyce paused in thought as she reminisced over her and Yarni's stormy relationship. "But we not talking about me. I do love her. Don't tell her I said it, but I love her like I would if I'd given birth to her myself."

"So she's nice."

"Sweet as pie until you do her wrong." Joyce shot Desember

a look. "Don't get on that woman's bad side, because she will have some shit for ya ass, now," Joyce warned Desember. "But you know what I love about her most? She loves your father and he loves her. Them two stick together like peanut butter and jelly. Always got each other's back."

Impressed, Desember nodded her head, thinking of her own relationship with Fame.

Fame and Desember had not been together even a year, but they had been through so much. The two of them had robbed, fought like cats and dogs and gone to jail together. It was only fitting that if he had to get shot, it would go down while they were together.

Joyce interrupted her thoughts when she noticed Yarni's car and said, "She's home, that's her car." She pointed to the platinum-colored GT Bentley.

But Desember's attention was on the chocolate-skinned guy at the door. He was handsome and dark-skinned with thick wavy hair. "So that's what I would have looked like had I been a boy," she mumbled, noticing that Des had some of the exact same features as she did.

Joyce heard Desember's comment and then followed her eyes to Des standing in the doorway. "Told you, you are the spitting image of him."

Des walked down the steps of the porch to the back of the Benz. She thought he would have spoken to her but he seemed to be focused on getting the bags in. He tapped the trunk with the heel of his hand, so Joyce would pop the latch from the inside. Once it rose, he grabbed two of the half-dozen pieces of luggage and headed inside the house.

A little girl ran past Des as he was hauling the first load of bags inside. She took off running toward Joyce, yelling, "Grandma!"

Joyce gave the little girl a huge hug, picking her up from the ground. Desember knew this had to be Desi, her baby sister.

"Ya-Ya!" Desi called out.

Joyce gave Desi a kiss on the forehead. "Girl, you getting heavy. Ya-Ya not gonna to be able to pick you up if you keep growing like a weed."

"I don't plan to stop growing anytime soon. Mommy says I'm going to be taller than her," Desi informed her grandmother.

"Hi, Desi," Desember greeted, and she felt a connection the moment their eyes locked.

"I know who you are," Desi said, pointing to her older sister.

"Who am I?" Desember asked with a wide smile.

"Your name is Desember, like the month." Her eyes danced. "And you might be my big sister."

Growing up an only child, Desember always imagined what it would be like to have a brother or sister. "That's right," she said, "I might be your big sister."

"Desi, come in here with no coat on," Yarni yelled from the doorway. When Desi hesitated, Desember whispered, "Do what your mommy tells you," she instructed her sister.

"I will show you where your room is," Desi said, then took off skipping into the house. There was a vibe in the air that let Desember know that house rules as she knew them were about to change. She was no longer living with a passive mother who let her have her way. Her room? Baby sister? Dad? Stepmonster? She had a lot of things to try to get used to.

9

DNA

When Desember walked inside the house, it didn't disappoint, the interior was like an episode of *MTV Cribs*. There were two separate spiral staircases, columns and a colossal fireplace, burning what looked like a half a tree chopped up in four pieces.

"Hi, Desember, welcome to Virginia. How was your journey in?" Yarni was trying to be nonchalant but cordial. But it wasn't easy downplaying how much the girl indeed resembled Des.

"The ride and company were cool," Desember answered, somewhat uncomfortably. But she really didn't know what else to say. She was trying to ear-hustle the conversation that Joyce and Des were having in the foyer, but from the great room, where she and Yarni were, it was next to impossible to do.

"Do you have to be cold?" Joyce asked her son.

"I don't know the girl," Des said defensively, "What do you expect?"

"Act like you care. That's what I expect. Make the chile feel warm in your house."

There was a moment of silence between Joyce and Des, and during it Yarni asked, "Would you like some hot chocolate?"

"If it's not too much trouble." Desember took her coat off. "It's cold as hell out there."

"It's cold as what?" Des said, dropping the last of the bags in the foyer.

"My bad. Didn't mean to cuss," Desember apologized. "It's a bad habit of mine."

"Not everybody in here is grown." Des gestured toward Desi. "That's our daughter, Desi, and I'm Des—from what I've been told, I could be your father." Des nodded toward Yarni. "And you've met my wife. This is going to be kind of awkward for us all for a while, you, me and Yarni. But we gon all figure it out and be one happy family, if you're truly my daughter."

Yarni intervened because she wanted this transition to be as comfortable and easy as possible for both Des and Desember. She knew that Des was playing it low key for her sake, so she decided to take on the role of peacemaker. "Before we get into all that, do you need me to show you to your room to get comfortable? Or you want to just chill out here while I make the hot chocolate?"

Fuck the hot chocolate and the bullshit, Desember thought to herself but responded, "Do you all have a computer down here that I could use?"

"Yes, we keep a laptop in the library," Yarni answered. "Let me get the hot chocolate started and then I'll show you where it is."

After Yarni put the milk on the stove, Desember followed her to the library. Yarni directed her to a glass desk and an iBook.

"Thanks. Can you ask Des to join us, please?" Desember asked.

"Sure." Yarni went to get him.

By the time Desember had the computer up and running, Des and Yarni had come into the room.

"What can I do for you?" Des asked Desember, his arm around Yarni's waist. "My wife said you wanted her to come get me."

"Give me a second." Desember's fingers were busy tapping the keys on the keyboard and then they came to a stop. "I just need a credit card from you," she said.

She caught him off guard. "It's a lil fast to be going shopping, don't you think?" he said with a smile. "You've only been here two minutes."

"I'm going to keep it real with you. My mother has a track record of not being totally honest when it comes to paternity issues. Although your mother says she can look at me and tell I'm yours, I would like to be sure. I'm sure you don't want to waste your time taking care of a child that ain't yours. Before I get into your world or I let you into mine, there is one important matter of business that needs to be resolved. This has to be done now, time is the most precious commodity we have and I don't want you to waste any of mine nor yours. I'm ordering a paternity test so we all can be clear of what's what."

Des nodded at the girl's logic and went in his wallet, handed over his credit card and watched her finger the numbers in. He'd been planning to get around to that eventually anyway. After the punching of a few final keys, she handed the card back to him. At that moment Des felt guilty about how he initially came off; all Desember wanted to know was the truth. Same as everybody else. "I apologize if I offended you, but this is the first time I've had to deal with something like this."

Desember snapped off, "So, I'm the only daughter you've ever abandoned?"

"Look, I met your mother like twenty years ago, during bike week. She was in college, out for spring break." He looked at Yarni then back to Desember. They both were all ears. "We got hot and heavy right off the bat." He made sure to clarify. "This was before I ever met my wife. But after the weekend I never heard from your mother again."

"Why wouldn't she try to contact you if she knew she was carrying your child?"

"Maybe I can answer that." All eyes were now on Joyce. She entered the room carrying a Heineken and a sheepish expression.

They all stared transfixed as they waited for her to go on.

"Angie had a boyfriend back at school when she met Des," Joyce began. "Her mother convinced her that the baby could have been either of theirs. Why stir up unnecessary trouble?" Joyce paused to take a deep breath before continuing. "After the baby was born—actually, after you were around two years old, your features became more defined. Angie knew in her heart that the baby belonged to you, Des. She looked up my number and contacted me."

"Why didn't you call me?" Des asked, shocked by the story.

"Because you had gotten locked up by that time," Joyce said, "that's why." She shot him a look. "Now be quiet and let me finish what I was saying. I don't know why you don't exercise your manners after all that home training I gave you."

"Okay, Ma, go ahead," Des gave in.

"Thank you." Joyce rolled her eyes. "As I was about to say," she continued, "I told her you were found guilty of a horrible crime that you didn't commit and the judge sentenced you to an unimaginable amount of time."

Joyce addressed Desember. "Angie told me all about you, Desember. She was almost certain you belonged to my son. I offered to take you," Joyce gave a caring smile to Desember, "and raise you myself. But Angie wasn't having it. And I couldn't blame her. I was being selfish because I'd just lost my son to the system and I wanted someone to fill the empty space I had in my heart.

"Angie said she didn't want her baby to come up with a father who was behind bars all his life. It wasn't fair to the child." Joyce took a sip of her beer. "Not to say that I agreed with her, but it was her child, not mine, so all I could do was follow her wishes. Angie made me promise I would keep her secret. And for my silence she periodically called me through the years, to fill me in on how you were doing." Joyce couldn't help staring at this young woman who was her granddaughter. "I always sent presents at Christmas and your birthday, and cash every month to help out."

Desember pushed a tear away. This was her first time hearing the intimate details. Her mother was in such a rush to get her out of North Carolina to safety, she really didn't have time to go into everything in depth. "How come my mother still kept the secret once Des was out of prison?"

"I've said enough. I think you should take that one up with Angie."

"Well, the test will be here the day after tomorrow," Desember said, softly. "After we get the samples, it says, the results will be back in a week."

Stunned by the story Joyce had just told, Des tried to stay composed. "Regardless of what the DNA test says, you can stay here as long as you want. And if it turns out you are truly my daughter . . . then I got a lot of time to make up for, don't I?"

Desember had heard that bullshit before. She'd heard it many times before. Same story, different nigga—or should she say "different daddy"? There were tons of false promises that the other men accused of being, or pretending to be, her daddy, had made to Desember, so she didn't respond to his comment. Only time would tell.

10

Lunch with the Girls

In downtown Richmond, a small crowd had begun to gather at the Sugar Hill Café soul food eatery. It was the ideal spot for a quick meal with a home-cooked flavor. Sitting in one of the four large booths positioned in front of the window views of 2nd Street, Yarni checked e-mails from her cell phone. She was the first to arrive for the girls' lunch get-together. She'd thrown it together at the last minute for Bambi, Lava and herself to get to know Desember better and at the same time introduce her to a couple of key people in Yarni's life.

Besides, Bambi had called so many times, asking hundreds of questions about Desember, it was impossible for Yarni to get any work done. Actually, Bambi was the one who suggested introducing Desember to Lava, and Yarni thought it was a good idea.

Lava was only about two or three years older than Desember, so they should have a few things in common.

When Bambi pulled up she parked directly in front of the restaurant. She waved to Yarni, hit the button to lock the doors on her car, and then rushed to the entrance. They had different mothers, but besides one being a few shades of chocolate lighter than the other—Yarni more of a caramel color to Bambi's Hershey's chocolate skin tone—the half-sisters could've passed for twins.

Both were into fashion heavily, but Bambi was a true fashionista. This afternoon she wore skinny jeans tucked in the top of brown thigh-high stiletto boots, a cowl-neck wool sweater, and a waist-length leather jacket that matched her footwear. She blew through the door like a gust of fashionably fresh air. Quite a few sets of eyes followed as she made her way to the booth.

After a quick hug Bambi joined her sister in the booth. "So where's Des's grown daughter?" Bambi asked, not wasting any time.

Yarni got the waitress's attention before responding to Bambi. "Yo' ass is terrible," she admonished. "First of all, Soledad O'Brien, you got your reports wrong. Until it's confirmed by the paternity test, my naive sister, for now Desember is Des's alleged daughter, at best. And if you must know everything," she shared, "since I was coming from the office, I asked Lava to pick her up. They should be here any minute."

The waitress showed up like an exclamation to a point well made.

"Hi, I'm Cathy, your waitress today. Are you ready to order now?" the waitress asked, obviously in a hurry to get their order.

"Just drinks for now. We're waiting on two more people to join our party," Yarni told the waitress.

Cathy pulled out her pen. "Not a problem. What would you like to drink?"

Bambi ordered an apple martini and Yarni a grape-ade with a lime wedge.

Bambi turned her nose up at her sister. "You ain't drinking with me?" she asked, though she knew Yarni never drank alcohol during working hours. Yarni shot her a look, and then Bambi said, trying to mock her sister, "A clear head makes a clear decision. I know the speech."

As soon as Cathy was out of earshot, Bambi was back at it. "Do she look like Des?"

"Yes," Yarni hated to admit. "To be honest the girl looks just like him. I wanted to hate the lil heifer, but my conscience wouldn't go along with my heart."

"Damn, girl. If it makes you feel any better, I bet her mama's a dog." They burst into laughter. "A real pitbull," Bambi added, trying to mimic the expression of a menacing canine. Not even close.

Yarni knew Bambi was just trying to make her laugh to lighten the mood. And it was working—sort of. "Girl, have I told you lately how glad I am you're my sister?"

"Not lately, but don't worry—you can show me, because Christmas is coming soon."

They spent the next few minutes talking about Bambi and her husband, Lynx. Now that the focus was on her, Bambi came clean. They were far from broke but the recession had put a major dagger through her once lucrative party-planning business.

"People just ain't splurging like they used to," she said. "And mu'fuckers getting sheisty."

Yarni concurred. "Tell me about it," she said, thinking about the church robbery. Then suddenly something jarred her memory.

Yarni snapped her fingers, realizing the girl she'd talked with prior to church the morning of the robbery was with one of the robbers. "The stripper chick." Why hadn't she thought about that before? Had she been that devastated and afraid for her family's life that she'd forgotten all about something that significant?

Bambi was puzzled. "What stripper?" she asked visibly confused.

The scene ran through Yarni's head as clear as a YouTube clip. The first time the girl came to the church, Sister Mary was saying she'd heard that girl worked at that new high-dollar strip club.

$ $ $

"What girl is that?" Yarni asked, making polite conversation with the old-timer. Sister Mary was like Pearl from the old sitcom *227*. She didn't miss a beat when it came to who was doing what. Pointing to a pretty young lady wearing a tight dress, Sister Mary gave up the business.

"Roxanne is her name," Sister Mary said.

$ $ $

"There they go." Bambi gestured toward the front door when she saw Lava and the guest of honor come through it.

Yarni's thoughts traveled back to the present as they made their way over to the booth, trying to conceal conspiratorial smiles. Lava and Desember seemed to be getting along well, Yarni thought. Maybe a bit too well.

As soon as the girls reached the table Desember immediately started talking about the invitation she had gotten. Lava had invited Desember to a big party. After only being in the city for a couple of days, Desember wasn't sure how her "supposed" dad was going to react. She didn't want to ruffle any feathers, but Lava made the party sound irresistible.

Yarni introduced Desember and Bambi. "I love it down in N.C.," Bambi said when she found out Desember was from North Carolina. "I put a few nice events together down there."

Lava and Desember talked to Bambi for a split second and then went back to the party chitchat. It was no secret both girls were excited about the upcoming event.

They all ordered: Yarni, spaghetti and meatballs; Bambi, fried fish and shrimp; Lava, baked chicken; and Desember, the smothered pork chops. Five minutes or so after two of the entrees arrived at the table, Yarni got an urgent e-mail. Cathy had apologized on behalf of the cook for the extra time it was taking to complete the order.

"Damn, y'all!" She'd forgotten all about the meeting with the superintendent of the school board. Thank God for Layla. Yarni had almost blown a half-million-dollar account. "Sorry, girls, but I gotta go." She plucked a hundred dollar bill from her purse and laid it on the table. "This is for the food. Lunch is on me.

Call me later, sis. You two too," she said to Desember and Lava, "and try not to have too much fun."

"Aren't you at least going to get your food wrapped up to go?" Desember asked.

"Don't have time." Food was the last thing on Yarni's mind right now. Another round of good-byes and she was out the door.

Bambi looked at her watch, then placed three twenties of her own on the table. "I might as well take off too. I have millions of things to get done. Nice meeting you, Desember. Welcome to the family." She popped a shrimp in her mouth and was ghost.

When Cathy returned with the other two meals and the check, she asked, "Are they returning?" Her eyes were bouncing back and forth from where Yarni and Bambi had been sitting.

Desember took one look at her newly arrived meal and gasped. "I can't eat this," she complained. "It has onions on it."

"Yes, ma'am." Cathy sucked her teeth. "It's smothered with onions and gravy, the way you ordered it," she snidely added.

Desember's face was as tight as a Naomi Campbell weave. "The menu ain't say nothing about no damn onions. You can take that shit right back where you got it from."

Cathy didn't verbalize her displeasure, but it was obvious in her body language. She jerked the plate from the table, almost spilling it on Desember, and stomped off to the kitchen.

Lava dropped her fork in the center of her dish. "Let's get out of here, girl."

Desember didn't budge. "I'm not giving this bitch no hundred sixty dollars for some food nobody ate."

"You must'd misunderstood me, cuz. I said let's go, not let's pay."

Desember found an ink pen in her purse and for kicks they scribbled a note on a five-dollar bill. Courtesy of Lava.

$ $ $

The waitress was headed back to the table with the plate of food she had spit in, when she realized that the two girls were settling into a pearl white Lexus, giggling.

She was pissed because the four arrogant women had taken up the booth space for almost an hour. Too bad, she'd been looking forward to serving the loudmouth one pork chops with no onions but warm spit mixed in the gravy. When Cathy picked up the five-dollar bill she noticed the writing on it.

The script read:
You eat it,
And next time have
Better manners!
Beyatch!

11

Fantasy Island

The evening had dragged along like a snail hungover on an extra-salty margarita. Yarni just hadn't been able to get the girl—Roxanne—out of her head since lunch. So much so, she called Bambi and convinced her to meet at the Fantasy Island strip club at nine.

"And why are we here again?" Bambi asked when they hooked up in the parking lot of the club.

"Because I think one of the chicks who works here might know something about what went down at the church. I saw her with one of the robbers right before church service that day."

"Stop me if I'm wrong, but didn't them boys have machine guns? Why don't you let Des and dem deal with this?" Bambi asked.

"Because I don't know if she really knew what was going on, that's why. And if I tell Des, it may not matter—her ass will be grass."

"Oh okay, so we here because you feel some type of compassion for this girl?"

"Yeah, basically." Yarni thought about it. "But I do feel sorta bad also for not mentioning this to Des."

"You better than me, girl. But I guess, as crazy as it sounds, we are doing the right thing. I just hope this chick appreciates the favor you doing for her." Bambi knew the girl probably wouldn't understand that they were actually preserving her life by not first telling the boys what they knew, but she was only there to watch her sister's back.

The sisters entered Fantasy Island, for the first time.

The Fantasy Island Gentlemen's Club was where the upscale and wealthy went to unwind. It was a private club and management was very selective about the people they let in. The cover charge for men to get in was $250 with a kickback of $50 in drink coupons. However, female customers paid $350 without the kickback.

"As much as it costs to get up in this bitch, we better find out something," Bambi bitched.

"It's a gamble, I know." Yarni wasn't even sure if the girl really worked here. But she was willing to bet her money on Sister Mary's word. She just hoped that the mystery girl would be cooperative when they found her.

Once they had their hands stamped, they proceeded down a corridor called the International Hall as directed. The hall, which led to the main club, was lined with huge glass cages. They were all connected, but each was separated by partitions like one would see in a museum. And each had an opening designed for tips to be slid in.

"Damn, this shit is fly." Bambi looked around the club in awe at how laid out it was. It truly was like a mini fantasy world nestled in the outskirts of the city.

"It is," Yarni admitted. "They are cashing in off the oldest profession in the book." And in the next breath, she advised her sister, "You need to get the guy's card who owns this place. I could see you planning a hell of a bachelor party here."

"Me too, but let's focus on what we're here for."

As they strolled down the International Hall, every glass cage had a girl's name and what country she originated from. There was a look only, no touching policy for these girls, but if a patron wanted a private dance, he could get it by dropping a minimum of a hundred dollars in the cage. After doing so he would put on headphones that rested in front of the window, prompting the girl's theme music to automatically come on for her to dance to in a fashion indigenous to her country. It was customary that the gentleman would tip her while she danced. Other bypassers could tip her without hearing the music. It was a creative and innovative idea, and it worked.

Seeing the women from around the world decked out in their native but skimpy costumes was intriguing. Both Yarni and Bambi admired the thought put into creating this gentlemen's experience as they surveyed the glass cubicles. They saw a Moroccan belly dancer, a girl from Switzerland looking like she was about to yodel, a dark-skinned Nigerian girl who could have been a model, a Japanese geisha and a Tahitian treat.

"Damn, this shit is entertaining. I'm about to get me a dance," Bambi said, distracted by a sexy Indian girl with a red dot on her forehead doing an exotic Bollywood dance.

"Girl, how about we get what we came here for first," Yarni said. Her eyes caught sight of a woman dressed in a burka. At first all that could be seen were her eyes, then she started undressing, seductively. It didn't matter what the name of the god her admirers prayed to was, they unanimously agreed she was divine.

"Okay, now I got why people say this ain't your average strip club. It really isn't."

They spotted a room with a sign over the top that read, "Welcome to Atlanta," and they could hear Young Jeezy's song "Make It Rain" playing as they walked in. This was obviously where the club kept the big booty black girls with bodies like superheroes. There were a couple of big spenders flipping money around like it was counterfeit.

A girl that had to be at least six feet tall wearing a shirt that read *These are my real boobs* walked over and greeted them. "Welcome to Atlanta. I'm sorry, but it's a private show. A lucky man has rented the entire city."

"There's no way we can get in?" Yarni asked. She wanted to be sure Roxanne wasn't inside before they left.

"Sorry." The girl shook her head. "Not for at least another two hours. But I assure you there are some dynamite acts in other parts of the club."

"Well, we'll have a drink and be back, but if you can get us in sooner, we'd appreciate it." Yarni handed the amazon chick a crisp Franklin. The girl took the money but looked at her like she'd been insulted. Yarni's ego was bruised a bit because she could usually persuade a pitbull off a meat truck. "Damn, am I losing my swag?" she asked her sister.

"Naw, we just out our lane, that's all," Bambi said. Exotic dancers ran the entire place.

They took a seat in the main forum and ordered a drink. "Do you see her?" Bambi asked, as Yarni scanned the club. "Because this doesn't look like the right place—excuse me, the right part of the world we're in."

"I know she works here. At least that's what Sister Mary told me. Now, how she knows that's probably another story. It seems like the only black chicks—well, American ladies—are in Atlanta, and Roxanne does have that stripper look."

Yarni was observing how the men were going crazy.

"Well, all we can do is wait until Atlanta ain't under siege anymore," Bambi told her, then was distracted by the girl performing on the main stage. "Damn, look at that chick." Bambi was amazed at what the girl was doing. "That's talent, and please, by all means keep that hooker away from my man."

The girl was performing an acrobatic move that required a handstand and the flexibility of a rubber band. Then she rolled or tumbled, into a split.

Yarni stared at the young contortionist in awe, then, for the first time, she got a look at her face. "That might be our girl!"

"Damn, she musta been the Twister champ back in the day," Bambi said.

After getting a better look, Yarni was sure it was Roxanne and nodded her head in confidence, "That's her, that's Roxanne!"

When the waitress returned with their drinks, and Yarni asked her, with an extra forty-dollar tip, "Is there a way you can set up a VIP for us with her," she pointed to the stage, "Please?"

The waitress eyeballed the expensive clothes the two ladies were wearing, looked at Bambi, then back at Yarni. She tucked the two twenties into her bra. "It's possible, but I need a little more incentive." She cracked a greedy smile.

For a split second Yarni considered ringing the washed-up broad's neck, but she caught herself. Coming to the aid of her sister, Bambi handed the waitress another bill, this one a Franklin. "Now, make it happen." Bambi shot the girl a look as if to say, "And if you think you get one iron dime more than that, you must be smoking crack; you better be able to do some tricks or something."

The buck forty did the trick.

The two sisters were about to discuss the greedy waitress getting her hustle on when they were approached by a funny-looking, rail-thin black dude with high-water pants and round glasses. "You two look good," he complimented. "If you ever need a man to join your twosome, I'd love to be of assistance," he offered with a cigar hanging out of his mouth. "You won't be disappointed." He winked.

They shot him down in unison. "No thanks."

After he left, Bambi leaned in and said to Yarni, "Girl, they think we gay."

"Ahhh, yeah. Well, we are together at a strip club with female dancers," Yarni reminded her.

Just then the waitress returned with a guy wearing a tight black suit. He had no salutations for the sisters, just got straight down to business. "To VIP with Roxanne it's a thousand for one of you and five hundred for the other, plus tips—cash. But if you run it on your credit card, it's a twenty-five percent processing fee."

The lawyer in Yarni wondered if all that was legal, but her thoughts were interrupted when Bambi leaned in and whispered into her ear, "You still wanna save this bitch's life?"

"Stay focused, you know why we're here. Call it community service."

"A'ight, Captain Save-a-Ho, let's cough up the cash," Bambi said as she went into her purse. "I can contribute like three hundred. You know my husband got us in the poor house."

"Don't worry about it, I got it." Yarni peeled off fifteen big face Benjamins from the cash Tangaleena had given her. She was glad she hadn't had time to go to the bank and make a deposit.

Once they produced the money, the man gave someone else a thumbs-up, then directed Bambi and Yarni past a door that read "Red Light District." The other guy then led them to a door on which he simply placed his finger, and his fingerprint caused the door to unlock. This door led to a hallway with red carpet that had private rooms off to each side. Their temporary escort opened the door to room number four. He faced the two sisters with a stern face. "You have two songs," he said.

"That's all we get? What is that, like six minutes?" Bambi asked, feeling robbed without a gun.

The man looked at them and said, "Normally it's one song,

the man said, but since there are two of y'all, I'm being nice, allowing you two cuts. Just make sure you tip Roxanne good."

Yarni saw the expression on Bambi's face and quickly intervened. "Two songs is all we need. Thank you, sir." She gave him a look that said "Get the hell out so we can get this show on the road."

"Enjoy!" He flashed a fake smile as he started to exit the room. But before he left completely, he added, "Roxanne will be in shortly." He took his time standing there, like it was customary for people to give him a tip. But what he didn't have, he wouldn't get from them.

"This is some shit, you know that, right?" Bambi asked when he was finally gone.

"You mean it's the shit, or it's some shit?"

Before Bambi could answer, the door opened and Roxanne walked in. When she caught sight of Yarni she was a little confused and looked as if she'd seen a ghost or something. "Oh my God, First Lady, I wasn't expecting you and I know you wasn't expecting me either. Should I just leave and act like neither of us saw each other?" she asked. "I know it's awkward."

Yarni read the girl's face. Her eyes darting back and forth between Yarni and Bambi. That's when it dawned on Yarni what the young girl was thinking—that she was there with her lover. Yarni quickly corrected her. "No, this is my sister, and we are here to see you, Roxanne."

"Well, I'm one of the top girls here. If you want the cream of the crop, you got the right girl." She smiled, licking her lips.

"Not quite, honey," Yarni said in a tone as if to advise young missy to put on the brakes and not flatter herself. "Now, we did see you perform and you are very gifted." Yarni gave her the once-over. "And your outfit is very exotic." Roxanne had changed into a skimpy tiger print number.

"If you are not interested in having an 'experience,' then why are you here?" The girl, still in hustle mode, now grew suspicious.

"Because I wanted to talk to you about what happened on Sunday."

"Talk to me about what? I was there just like you were," Roxanne said nonchalantly, as if it was no big deal. "I got my shit stole just like everybody else. Now my ass gotta work overtime just to break even."

"Cut to the chase." Bambi was frustrated with the girl and knew the clock was ticking. "Look, ain't nobody here for no lap dances, no head or no pussy."

Roxanne got offended. "I don't give head."

"Okay, yeah right, whatever." Bambi rolled her eyes, knowing homegirl was damn lying. "Look, my sister is here because she's a compassionate type of person and she just paid over two G's to save your ass. So stop the bullshit."

"Save me from what? This club? The life that I'm living? You can't save me, because I don't want to be saved, not from all this cash I'm making. Within the next five years I'll be retired, with my white picket fence and doing whatever I want to do."

"No, honey, trust me, she's not here on no first lady missionary trip," Bambi corrected the girl.

"Look, I wanted to talk to you because on Sunday you were with one of the guys who robbed the church," Yarni said before Bambi's mouth took them two steps back.

"And?" Roxanne snapped. "I had no part of that madness."

"Right," Yarni said, studying the girl's eyes. "But you know something about it," she accused Roxanne in a firm tone. "You can either talk to me now or you can deal with the repercussions when my husband finds out different."

"And let me be the first to say that door number two is not going to go over well," Bambi added.

Yarni tried a different approach. "Let me ask you something, did you ever see the movie *Jaws*?"

"Yeah, I saw all of them. But what does that have to do with anything?" Roxanne asked.

"Look, basically, if you don't talk to me, I'm going to have to pass your name over to the sharks, and right now they are hungry for any information but *starving* to find anyone to get revenge, any way they can."

"This ain't no bullshit game and nobody's pulling your leg. My sister is only trying to help you," Bambi said.

Roxanne took in the words being spoken to her by the tag team pair. After thinking for a moment, she stated, "I was with the guy, but I didn't know him like that. I met him and we spent a few days together. I told him that I belong to the church. He told me he wanted to change his life around too. So I invited him to come."

"What's his name?"

"Dick."

Now they were getting somewhere.

"Last name?" Yarni drilled.

Bambi laughed. "That's some ole bogus name—you know that, right?"

Yarni elbowed Bambi because she knew that the drink she'd had was getting to her. She normally had a smart mouth, but tonight there was no stopping her. Yarni continued her line of questioning as if Roxanne was a witness on the stand. "Did you have a last name for Mr. Dick?"

The girl dropped her head. "I don't know it, though. And now that I think about it, he played me too."

"How?" Yarni asked.

"Because I had asked him when I first met him, which was like a month or two ago, to come to church. He kept making up excuses why he couldn't come that Sunday and then the next. Then out of the blue, the night before the robbery, he was suddenly all excited about going with me. We spent the night together. He'd happened to pack his suit and overcoat in his car. But when all that shit popped off at church, I was just as stunned as everybody else. And to top it all off, he took my purse too."

"Do you know where he's from?"

"No, I don't." She thought for a second. "I caught him in a lie, though. At first he said he was new to the area and he didn't know anyone here. Then he said he had a cousin that lived here. Besides that, I don't really know much about him."

"Are you sure?" Yarni pressed. "You don't remember anything at all? Like where he lives?"

"Nope, that's one of the reasons guys deal with us. We don't ask any questions. He was a big spender and I didn't want to drive him away." She was visibly disappointed at not being more help. "Damn, I feel horrible."

"Do you have a phone number for him?"

"I did, but when I tried to call him after the robbery, to ask him what the hell he was thinking, the number had been cut off. I mean like immediately."

Yarni wanted to take what the girl was saying at face value, but she knew she still couldn't trust her completely.

Roxanne must have sensed Yarni was still doubting her. "I promise you on my life that I didn't know anything like this was going to happen. Had I known, I would have never came over to talk to you or even brought him with me to church." She dropped her eyes, then immediately lifted them again, her face lighting up like a bright idea had just popped into her head. "Oh my goodness, I might have something."

"I'm listening," Yarni said.

"Well, the first night we were together, he made a call on my cell phone because his was dead. Whoever he called got mad because he'd used my phone. I could tell that much from the one side of the conversation I could hear. I remember the person getting mad and hanging up on Dick. He later told me it was his cousin."

"Well, can you call your cell phone provider and get the number? Go on the Internet and search for it or something?"

Roxanne shook her head in disappointment. "Nope, I have a prepay phone and I don't get a bill. They won't allow me to even see calls I've made."

"I might be able to legally get your phone records if you sign off on it." Yarni threw the statement out there more to see the girl's reaction than anything else.

"Okay, no problem. I'll sign whatever you need me to." She sounded sincere. "I really want you to catch him, because what happened was really fucked-up and I'm sure people in the church probably think I had something to do with it, but I honestly didn't. Besides, when you catch him, I may be able to get my purse back from him. It was a Gucci, not one of them knock-off joints either."

"Okay, first things first, let's get the number he called. I'll need you to come by my office to sign a release. If I'm not there, ask Layla, my legal assistant, for it." Yarni dug into her purse for one of her cards and handed it to Roxanne. "Here's my address and phone number."

"Not a problem at all. I'll come by tomorrow."

"Sorry to come to your job like this, but I had to find you. I wanted to talk to you before someone else in the church puts it together and passes you on."

"Believe me, I appreciate it." Roxanne cracked a warm smile to Bambi and then said to Yarni, "Do you mind if I ask for a favor? While you're here, and since you have a couple more minutes, would you mind saying a prayer with me before you leave?"

Bambi could not believe her ears nor her eyes when Yarni took both of their hands and began to pray. Upon Yarni's "Amen," Bambi remarked, "They ain't never lied when they said God is everywhere . . . even in a damn strip club."

"Amen to that," Yarni said, giving Roxanne a hug.

Street Royalty

If the crowd on the street was any indication, Scrooge had done it again. Ever since he'd gotten signed to a major record label, his name stayed ringing bells. He'd just released his new single and this was his third album release party in the city. The party was going down in the grand ballroom of Hotel Opulent. Lava finally found a spot on the third level of the parking deck to park her Lexus. After squeezing between two SUVs, she killed the engine and reached for her purse.

Desember pretended not to notice the pearl handle nine millimeter that Lava pushed to the side as she searched for her MAC lip gloss.

"Okay, lil cousin, there's a couple things you need to know."

"Like how to find the bar and dance floor?" Desember joked

in a real Southern drawl. "I know you think Flowerville's from another era but I've been in a club before."

They both laughed.

"Seriously, though," Lava gathered her composure, "you need to hear this. So listen good. Des is royalty in this town. Hated by some, loved by most, but respected by all. And just because I was engaged to his nephew, Nasir, I get treated like a member of the royal family."

"So you're the Duchess of Richmond?" Desember joked.

"Pretty much," Lava said without a second thought.

"Anything else I need to know?"

"Yeah, the shit may sound funny, but all jokes aside . . . ," Lava made sure she had Desember's full attention. "Des is your father. And you know what that means?"

Desember played along. "No, tell me."

"It means," Lava said, "whether you accept it or want it or not, that makes you the Princess. Once people find out, they gonna treat you different. For better or worse but mostly better. I just thought you should know. Now, once we in, don't leave my side—we go wherever together."

"Got ya. Now let's go into the damn party, please."

Before they could get inside, Desember peeped a few admirers checking them out.

"Damn, baby, you fine. Let me get a few minutes wit chat," cracked a guy in a blue mink jacket standing next to a black extended-length Escalade.

"You're not coming into the shindig?" Desember inquired as she kept walking.

With a slight smile, he replied, "Maybe a lil later, baby." He looked her up and down with lust in his eyes. "Definitely before they slice the birthday cake."

Lava pulled Desember ahead. "They from the 643, and dem dudes you don't want no parts of." She looked over her shoulder to double check that she was giving the proper information to her little cousin. The dude caught Lava looking and waved to her. Lava rolled her eyes and kept stepping while spilling the tea. "Yes, girlie, they into some shit. Always up to no good. As a matter of fact, if this wasn't *the* party of the year, I would leave at this very moment because whenever those clowns are around there's always some stupid shit that seems to follow them," Lava said.

"Lava, I like your friend," the guy in the blue mink called out.

The girls ignored him and kept it moving straight past the velvet ropes. They headed right into VIP checked, where there were bottles popping like asses in a rap video.

Lava hadn't lied: she knew everybody, and even though it wasn't her party, they were both treated like first-class street royalty. Desember loved every second of it. People came over, wanting to be introduced to her as she mingled with the who's who of the town. The DJ even gave them shout-outs on the mic. They were having a blast, and then the DJ began playing the instrumental to 50 Cent's "In Da Club," and the DJ started singing, "Go, Scrooge, it's your birthday!" The crowd went crazy. Scrooge got on the stage and was dancing with about ten half-naked girls dressed in blue and white fur minidresses. Then one of Scrooge's boys, who was drunk, took the microphone from the DJ and announced, "Wait until y'all see this motherfucking birthday cake!"

At that very second a fight broke out. At first, Desember was shielded from everything because she was in VIP, but in a matter of seconds, VIP had turned into a romper room. Every bouncer in the club was either running to or already caught up in the melee. Without security to stop them, people pushed their way into the VIP section to avoid getting hit. Others used the opportunity to help themselves to the bottles of champagne that were on display for Scrooge's very important guests.

The brawl took Desember by surprise but Lava acted quickly. She grabbed Desember's hand to guide her to the coat check. "The party is officially over for us. We got to get the hell outta here before they get to shooting."

"I'm following you," Desember said. She was forced to let go of Lava's hand when three bouncers flew in between them, almost knocking Desember down as they ran toward the fight.

When Desember caught up with Lava, she was talking to the coat check girl who was definitely upset about something or someone. It didn't take very long for Desember to find out why.

"Them fucking fools robbed the door and had the fucking nerve to take my got-damn tip jar. I needed that money to buy my baby some smoke when I leave here." Her makeup was smeared down her face from crying.

"Damn, girl." Lava really didn't give a used tampon about the tip jar. All she wanted to know was, "Do you know who it was?"

Just then, Desember's attention went down the hallway, out the door, where she saw a rack of coats being put into the black stretch Escalade she'd seen earlier. Never taking her eyes from the truck, she took off down the hall because she wanted to make sure that the thieves had not taken their coats. However, by the time she got to the entrance, the Escalade had peeled off, leaving a trail of smoke. She walked back down the hall, praying that maybe Yarni's coat had been spared. She shoved her claim ticket into the girl's hand. "Tell me them fools don't have my coat."

In her heart Desember knew the answer to the question but wanted to hear it from the horse's mouth.

The girl didn't even double check the ticket. "The stickup boys got you too."

Desember was outdone. As they walked to the car, all she thought about was how Fame's victims must have felt.

It ain't no fun when the rabbit's got the gun!

13

If It Wasn't For
Bad Luck

Desember sat in Lava's car, bent over at the waist, holding her head in her hands. She had a splitting headache. *This can't be happening* kept running through her mind. That, and how was she going to get that damn coat back.

"You okay, girl?" Lava's coat was also stolen and even though it was a present from Nasir, her dead fiancé, Desember seemed to be more distraught than she was. "The hoodlums in the big city shook you up, huh?"

Desember sucked her teeth at Lava. "Girl, not hardly. You don't know the half of my bio. I've seen far worse than a damn fight in a club. Trust me."

"I thought so," Lava said, obviously expecting Desember to respond. After a few moments of silence, Lava reminded her, "But you gotta remember, it's only a coat, and it can be replaced."

Desember looked up, "I know that! But it belonged to Yarni and I didn't even ask her permission to borrow it."

"Oh shit," Lava exclaimed. "Girl, that's *really* fucked-up!"

"Exactly." Desember shook her head from side to side, but she couldn't shake the mess she'd gotten herself into.

"It's already awkward enough that I showed up in these people's lives on some 'hello daddy dearest' type of shit. Like, I'm the daughter you never knew about. Oh, and I'm gonna need a safe place to chill out because some people who almost tried to kill my stickup kid boyfriend may have a hit on my life on too." She tried to make light of the situation.

"Damn." Lava hadn't looked at it from that point of view.

"But even though my entrance is bizarre and suspect, these people welcomed me into their world with open arms, giving me the run of the house. And as a thank-you, the first real time I'm out the house I betray their trust by borrowing a coat? And let some lames steal it." She sighed. "Like, for real, is this my life?"

"Damn, girl," Lava felt bad for her. "I don't know what to tell you, but I know I damn sure wouldn't want to be in yo' shoes right now. I heard Aunt Yarni used to be on some 'kick-a-bitch's-ass' back in the day. Don't let the power suits and briefcase fool ya!"

Desember was stressed and confused at the same time.

Lava didn't know how to help. "I'm not trying to be a bearer of bad news; I'm just giving you the real. I just want you to know what you're up against." When Lava turned the ignition, she saw the fuel level was low. "We gotta stop and get gas. If you want, we can go by the Waffle House too. Maybe some food will make you feel better and get your blood pressure down."

"What should I do?" Desember asked, unable to think about eating. "Do I just keep it real funky and tell her the truth?"

"That you stole her chinchilla and now it's probably going to be on the back of some D-boy's bitch?" Lava took her eyes off the road for a split second to look at Desember. "What if it was an anniversary gift from Des or has some sentimental value?"

Once Lava broke it down like that, Desember realized that telling Yarni probably wasn't her best option. Then another idea popped into her head: "We gotta buy it back."

"Yeah, that might work," Lava said. But then she thought about it further. "But it's not even going to be on the market for at least day or so, if at all—that coat could get one of dem niggas a ticket to plenty of pussy or props with a chick, so he might not want to sell it."

"Yeah but stealing coats . . . you gotta be strapped for cash!" Desember knew that was a desperate move.

"It would be the shock of the century if they were strapped for cash." Lava hated to be the bearer of bad news, but—"I don't think they're really pressed for the money—those stupid-ass 643 guys do that kind of shit for a sport."

When Lava pulled into the parking lot of the 24-hour Exxon gas station on West Broad Street, Desember saw something that caused her to eyes to pop. "You see what I see? That's the truck dude and 'em was riding in. The same one I seen 'em put the coats in."

The Escalade was parked off to the side of the gas station, near the air pumps.

"Lava, ain't that dat dude tried to holla at me?" She pointed at the guy wearing the blue mink, strolling inside the store part of the Exxon.

"Yup, it sure is." Lava nodded with a smile. "Damn, lil cuz, our luck may be turning around. But wait a minute, how we gonna get him to give it back?"

"Whatever we do, we gotta figure this shit out real quick while this dude is in the store. You know him, right? And do you think I'll be able to sweet-talk him out of it?" Desember asked, speaking fast.

"I only know of him. And he's a fucking asshole in his own way, so I wouldn't roll the dice on that sweet-talk plan. Dem dudes don't respect no chick. They only respect the code of the streets."

"A'ight, then, I know his kind." She nodded. "Then we gotta keep it moving to plan B, which is a little mo risky business! You got my back?"

Lava looked at her like she was crazy, almost taking the question as an insult.

"I'm going to take that as a yes."

"You ain't even gotta ask. Now, what we going to do?"

"After I do what I gotta do, I'm going to need you to lead me outta here. I don't have the foggiest idea where I'm at. A'ight, we gotta move pretty fast." She spoke rapidly.

Before Lava could protest or agree, Desember was making moves like she did this type of thing all the time.

"I know you ain't thinking about doing what I think you thinking 'bout doing."

"Nope," Desember said. "I'm done thinking about it. I'ma take the truck. Now ride or die with me, cuzo." Then she was moving faster than a gazelle in the jungle.

Desember was prepared to bust the windows out and hotwire the car if she had to, but lucky for her the door to the Escalade was unlocked. *These fools even left the keys in the ignition,* she thought to herself. She was at the point of no return.

Desember quickly rammed the gearshift in reverse, spun the truck around, and rolled out like she was the repo man. The Escalade had so much horsepower that at first she was close to being on two wheels, which wiped the smile right off of her face.

In the rearview mirror someone was running after her, waving his hands like that would make her stop. Not hardly. Once the Escalade straightened up, she mashed the accelerator of the eight cylinders as hard as she could to get the hell out of Dodge. It only took a few seconds for her to adjust, and then she was the one in control of the the truck and the situation.

The rush, at the moment, had her feeling like she was higher than any drug could make her. Lava trailed behind in full throttle, passing the truck so Desember could follow her. Desember called Lava on her cell phone. "Girl, I know you still need gas but you gotta take us somewhere safe, first."

"A'ight." Lava was giggling. "But, bitch, you crazy as shit."

"You didn't know," Desember agreed, feeling a rush from the adventure.

They finally pulled over in an apartment complex to search the back of the Escalade. They found Lava's fur, but Yarni's coat wasn't there and Desember started to freak out.

Desember searched again and again. "If it wasn't for bad luck, I swear I wouldn't have any luck at all."

That's when they heard a phone ring. "Is that your phone?" Lava asked.

"Nope, you know good and well I wouldn't have no damn booty pop song as no ringtone." Desember continued to check the coats, for the sixth or seventh time. "The shit has to be here," she mumbled.

The ringing came from the front seat of the Escalade. Lava answered the phone, "Hello."

"Where the fuck you at?" Dude sounded mad.

Lava passed the phone to Desember.

"Hello, who is speaking and what do you want?" Desember toyed with the caller, knowing good and well who it was.

"Don't play games, bitch! You know who it is. Why you take my shit?"

"Wait one minute. You can kill that 'bitch' shit right now, *motherfucker*!" Desember said into the phone, clearly not intimidated. "And I could ask the same damn question: why you take my shit? And where the fuck is my chinchilla?"

"I thought that was you. You the girl I tried to holla at outside."

"Well you got my attention now. So holla. Where's my shit?"

"Tell me where you are and we can talk about it."

"Outside in the cold, with no damn coat, that's where," she said.

"Look, baby, we got off on the wrong foot. My name is Rocko and I apologize for any inconvenience, but we can get this shit all figured out. Take what's yours. Then tell me where you are."

"First of all," Desember said, "my fucking coat isn't here. And secondly, why in the hell would I tell you where I am?"

"I respect yo gangsta, Ma. But you said yo'self, the coat ain't there. What you want me to do?"

"What I want," Desember informed him, "is for you to get my shit back. However you do that is your choice. Hook or crook. I really couldn't give a damn."

"This is what I'ma gonna do," Rocko said. "And this is because I like you. I'll try to get with my boy and hopefully find you your coat. No promises. But don't let nothing happen to my truck, or there's going to be problems."

"In case you haven't figured it out yet, Rocky—"

"It's Rocko," he corrected her.

"Well, Rocko, we already got problems, and I ain't much for talking about them unless you get my coat. I'll be waiting on you." She hung up. He called right back and she answered. "Don't call this phone anymore until you got my damn coat, okay?"

"Right, I got that, but you got shit that belongs to me as well, and I need to get my truck back. How long you going to be up?"

"I'm up and out. I'm not going home without my coat. Basically it's like this: ain't no sleep for the weary—and if I don't sleep, guess what, champ? You won't either! Call me back when you got my coat in your hand. Until then, I'm joyriding on your full tank of gas, smoking all of your weed that you had in the glove box, and you better hope I don't fuck up your rims when I bend the corner or park this big boy shit here." Desember disconnected the call and sat in the driver's seat and rolled them a big fat spliff courtesy of Rocko as she faced reality.

It was after 3 a.m., and she had passed her curfew. She was in possession of a stolen truck filled with stolen furs and had no idea when, if ever, she would get Yarni's coat back. Saying she was in deep shit was truly an understatement.

14

A Blast from the Past

The next day Yarni was in her office, going over files, when Layla came over the intercom: "You have a Ronald Bledsoe to see you. He says it's urgent." Layla dropped her voice to almost a whisper, "But don't they all say that?"

Yarni hadn't heard that name since God knows when. "What's it in reference to?"

"He says he's an old friend and needs to speak to you about a family issue. That's all he would tell me. I tried to get as much information as I could out of him. I placed him in the conference room for now, but if you want, I'll get rid of him."

When he mentioned family, was he there because he knew something about who shot Des? The robbery? Whatever the reason, her curiosity was definitely piqued. "No problem. I'll give him five minutes of my time in the conference room. Please interrupt in five minutes exactly."

"Of course." Layla knew the drill. Part of her job was rescuing her boss from people who wasted her time or wanted her legal advice for free. Yarni was guilty too; she was a caring person to a fault at times and got caught up in wanting to assist clients however she could. As Yarni made her way to the conference room, Layla set her alarm so that her boss would not fall victim to another joker.

The conference room was of moderate size on the second floor of the three-level building. Equipped with a legal pad and her favorite pen, Yarni walked into the room. Upon sight, she was surprised at the person who was sitting at the table. She had to do a double take to recognize him. Rahllo?

He'd lost at least fifty pounds. Maturity had suited him well. His skin tone, still black as midnight, had a radiance to it. The last time she'd seen him, they were at a club and he was feeling the effects of the laxative she'd slipped him. It was hilarious.

"Rahllo, talk about a blast from the past. The last time I saw you, you were a shitty mess in the worst way."

He stood and greeted her with a peck on the cheek. "Yeah, I was." He didn't put much into the comment. "But you still looking good, girl. Real good," he said as he stepped back to get a better view. "It's been such a long time."

"It has," she said. "How can I help you?"

The brightness in his eyes dimmed a few watts. "I don't want to waste your time, so I'm going to get right down to the point. I need your help," Rahllo said concisely, and looked into Yarni's eyes.

She knew that this had to be serious because the egotistical self-centered Rahllo she remembered would never admit needing anybody's help. Especially a woman—and her, to boot. Things must be real bad for him to come crawling to her. "How so?"

"I never really get into kids' business, but you remember my son, Rocko?"

"Of course." Yarni remembered him; she and his mother had had a couple run-ins back in the day.

"How is he?" she asked.

"You know he was just a little boy when you and I was dating. Well, he ain't no little nigga no more. He pushing twenty, but doing big boy shit in a grown man way. To make a long story short," Rahllo said proudly, poking out his chest, "he picked up where I left off, running these streets like crazy." He shook his head. "But I think he took to the streets at a younger age than I did," he boasted.

Surely this dude didn't show up at my place of business after almost twenty years to tell me his son is walking in his footsteps as a criminal, she thought, but asked, "Did he get locked up?"

"No, but from what I can gather, he had a run-in with your niece last night."

"What? My niece?" He had to be mistaken but in her heart Yarni knew he wasn't. All she could think about were those sneaky smiles that Lava and Desember both wore at lunch a few days ago.

"Well, Rocko said it was your niece that was Nasir's girl. But to be honest, there was another girl was with her and that's the chick that he really had the run-in with."

Yarni was surprised—but then again, she wasn't. Her gut feeling from the start told her that Desember was a little hellion. And she had bucked her curfew, had not made it in last night.

For a split second Yarni thought about the conversation she and Des had earlier that morning about Desember staying out all night long.

$ $ $

"So what you going to do about your daughter bucking curfew?"

"I'm going to deal with her whenever she get her ass back in this house."

"Her first time out she disobeys your rules, just wait until she gets comfortable."

"Don't get worked up about Desember. I got her," Des said, as if talking about it to Yarni was frustrating. She shrugged it off, because after all it was his alleged child, not hers—and as far as she was concerned it was his worry, not hers.

But boy was she wrong; the girl's trouble had been dropped in her lap now, she thought, and realized she had to iron out this girl's B.S.

"What exactly happened?" Yarni asked.

"Apparently, Rocko and his boys hit the coat check and robbed the door of some party last night, and the girls' furs were caught up in the process. Then as fate would have it, they saw the lil nigga at the gas station and jacked him for his truck." Rahllo shook his head with a slight smile. He was still in disbelief that the girls caught his son slipping as he continued to tell his son's side of the story to Yarni. "After she didn't find her coat with the others, she told him that she'd be holding on to the truck until Rocko comes up with her shit."

"So let me get this straight, the girls took your son's truck because he stole their jackets."

Rahllo nodded. "Pretty much."

Yarni was sure that there was something to this made-for-TV story being left out, and she intended to find out what it was.

"This doesn't seem like a terribly difficult problem, Rahllo. I mean, even for the young ones to work out." Before he could answer, she continued, "It seems to me that the kids can work it out amongst one another. He wants his car, and she wants her coat. Now, correct me if I'm wrong, but in our books fair exchange has never been robbery. "

"No doubt," Rahllo agreed. "But things have gotten a little more complicated. The coat went somewhere else and Rocko is still working to get it back. He's offered to pay the full price plus an inconvenience fee for her trouble, but he has to have the truck back ASAP."

Yarni surmised that they were getting closer to the real reason for his visit. "Why would Rocko be in such a hurry to shell out more than the coat is even worth?" she asked, trying hard not to sound like she was cross-examining him, but she was ready to go in on him hard because she still knew he was bullshitting her.

"You were always quick on your feet, Yarni. A brother man can't get too much past you." She could tell he was trying to figure out how much information he wanted to disclose. "Well, let's just say, the Escalade has a few added amenities that greatly increased the book's street value."

The foolishness had gone on long enough. "Cut the bullshit, Rahllo. What's in that truck?"

She could see his brain working overtime. Then he finally said, "A large quantity of heroin. There's close to five hundred thousand dollars' worth of dope in a stash spot, and we have to have it back."

Her first thought was Rocko had to be the dumbest guy in the world to go rob a coat check with a half million of dope in the car. Was he auditioning for a show called *The Dumbest Dickhead*? But that was neither here nor there—the dope was still missing. Rahllo wasn't the most violent person, but half a million had a tendency to bring the worst outta a person.

"Out of respect for you and Des, I come to you, to try to resolve this civilly."

Let the truth be told, Rahllo feared Des. And if he knew the girl with Lava was Des's daughter, he'd probably shit a brick.

Yarni listened as Rahllo went on, "But the real problem is that I put my ass on the line and got a bunch of D on consignment for Rocko."

"For your son, Rahllo?" she questioned. "Come on, now!" Yarni had heard it all. "Rahllo, you know better than that. That's utterly ridiculous. For your son?" she repeated.

"Fuck it, he going to do it anyway. I don't want my son getting fucked up in the game and niggas robbing him with high-ass prices. So if he gonna throw bricks, I'm going to make sure that it's well worth the risk."

She shook her head. "This is a conversation for another day, Rahllo."

"Spare me your lectures today." He reiterated, "I need to get that Escalade out of the girls' possession because they riding around hot as hinges on Hell's gates, and I'm pretty sure they don't even know it."

Before she could respond, Layla came in and reminded Yarni that her next appointment had arrived.

"Give us a couple more minutes."

"Yes, ma'am." Layla closed the door behind her.

"Look," Rahllo said, "I need you to get in touch with your niece and let them know we need to get the truck back from her and I will make sure she gets her coat in return or more than enough cash to replace it."

Yarni wanted to say she heard him the first time but she didn't. Instead, she took a few moments to contemplate the entire situation.

Before she could speak, he did: "I would hope that you'd do it on the strength of all the paper you got from me back in the day, but if not I will hire you for your services."

"That won't be necessary. No promises, but I'll see what I can do. Just give me a few hours to try and get to the bottom of this craziness. Leave me a number where I can reach you."

"It would be greatly appreciated if we could make the exchange today. And maybe," he threw it out with a stupid grin on his face, "I can persuade you to let me take you to dinner once the business is in order."

"Rahllo, my husband would kill you."

"Yeah, I know. But nothing wrong with me trying my hand—at least I'd go a happy man with a full stomach."

The second Rahllo left the office, Yarni snatched up the phone and dialed Des.

"I'm glad I caught you," she said when he answered.

"Hey, baby. I'm walking into a meeting right now. I'm going to have to call you back." He rushed her off the phone before she could get out another word. Just said, "Love you!" and was gone.

She tried to control her frustration by taking a deep breath, then dialing Desember. No luck there, the call went straight to voicemail. Same thing with Lava's phone. *Young women today,* she thought, remembering when she was the same way. She hoped that Desi would grow up with a little more sense. She then texted both girls.

I need you to call me—heard what happened last night—CALL ASAP!

Thirty minutes went by with no response from either of the girls. Yarni was getting more pissed with every minute that went by. And added to her frustration, Des had still not called her back. *No more Mrs. Nice Bitch,* she thought to herself before punching out another text message to the girls.

CALL ME BEFORE I BEAT BOTH OF YOUR ASSES! THIS IS NOT A JOKING MATTER! CONFIRM YOU WILL BE HERE BY 3PM!

Ten minutes later her BlackBerry buzzed a return message:

We will be there at 2:30 to tell you our side. It's not what you think! SORRY AUNTIE! The text was from Lava.

2:30 it is, see you then. She sat back in her chair and wondered what in the hell had she gotten herself into.

15

What Do We Know?

With five acres of pure unadulterated automobile opulence, Des's Grown-Man Toy Store was arguably the most fashionable and upscale spot on the East Coast to buy, or accessorize, a whip.

A maze of aisles, between bumper-to-bumper BMWs, Mercedes, Jaguars, Lexuses, Audis, Porsches and Range Rovers eventually led to a huge air-conditioned warehouse that housed only the best of the best exotic vehicles—from Lamborghinis to Ferraris to vintage classics. All roads led to the most important place on the lot, the main building, where the business and negotiations went down.

Inside the main building was a six-car showroom, and off to the right of a rose-colored Maserati a hallway opened to a full-service espresso machine with bottled waters stacked from floor to ceiling. About fifty feet past a station to make coffee and tea, the hall came to an abrupt end at a solid oak door. Behind that door, an important meeting was in progress.

Des sat behind a grand mahogany desk. "What have we found?" he asked his trusty men. He was tired of being on the defensive; it was time to get active and find out anything that would lead him to the people responsible for trying to take his life and the empire he'd built.

On the other side of the room Slim and Stanka sat on a leather sofa. Mo sat in one of the oversized chairs to the right of the sofa, and Black Bob, head lowered in his hands, sat in the one to the right. Chip stood nervously in the corner. He was raised in the hood but he wasn't a street dude by a long shot. Not like the others. His expertise lie in computers, and with a bachelor's degree in progressive finance, it was natural for him to take on the role of treasurer. Although when those two gunmen held a nickel-plated pistol to his dome and forced him to wire away Des's money with the click of a button, it was a job he probably wished he never had.

"Don't everyone speak at once," Des said after receiving no response. He knew that Black Bob was still mourning the death of his little brother, Tony. Shit, everybody was feeling the loss. Des had known the brothers since grade school. They were two neglected kids with a chip on their shoulders, and Joyce had basically taken them in once she found out their mother cared more about drinking than feeding her kids.

Stanka was the first to shoot his opinion into the fire. "I think they may've been from out of town." He looked up. "If it was local, it would've gotten out."

Des hadn't known Stanka as long as the others, but he trusted Yarni's uncle and valued his wisdom.

"I'm not too sure about that," Slim disagreed.

Des didn't believe the gunmen were from out of town either, but he held his theories to himself, for now.

"Why, Slim?" Des pushed his oldest and closest friend to continue.

"They were too comfortable," Slim said with his fingers fixed under his chin like a steeple. "When a person is in a strange city doing dirt, I don't care how smooth they are, there's a certain amount of nervous energy that surrounds them. It's as common as liquor stores in the hood."

Des nodded.

Black Bob raised his head. His eyes looked cold and hard. He spoke with the soft, deliberate timbre of a man that had seen more than his fair share of violence. "I don't give a fuck where they from. But the nigga that killed my lil brother, Tony— wherever I find 'im, that's where he's going to die. I put that on my mother's grave," he promised.

"I don't like all this mystery shit." Mo rose from the chair and started pacing. He preferred using his hands more than his head. A vein the size of a slug pulsated from the side of his neck. "I'm so frustrated I can't even think straight." He shook his head. "And the fact that shit went down in front of our very eyes and there wasn't anything we could have done is really fucking with me."

Des didn't have Mo on the team for his intellect anyway. The man was a certified stone-cold killer. He wasn't complicated—

in fact, pure and simple, he was a man-eating tiger, loyal to the hand that fed him.

"Then I'll do the thinking for the both of us," Des said to his friend. He made eye contact with Stanka, Black Bob, Chip, Slim and Mo before continuing. "I believe the same person, or people, that took the shot at me on Friday was behind the sting on the church. It's a strong gut feeling."

"But what does that tell us?" Slim asked. "We don't know who did that either."

"If they were willing to kill me, then it couldn't have been all about the money," Des said.

Stanka asked, "Why don't you think it was about the paper? These clowns got away with at least ten mil and that ain't even counting the congregation's money. What other reason would they need?"

"That's the point. If that shot they took hadn't hit the Bible, I'd be dead. And if they'd killed me on Friday, it would'na been nobody at the church to rob on Sunday. This shit is more about me than money or anything else." Des paused for a second. "Somebody either wants me dead or broke. It's just that simple."

Des had their undivided attention.

He was sure this was personal. He'd run the probabilities and possibilities over and over, and at the end he had to go with his gut.

"Now all I have to do is figure out who hates me enough that they would want to see me dead and risk the chance of losing out on a ten-million-dollar come-up?"

"That's like trying to find a needle in a haystack," Mo said.

"Exactly. The good thing about finding a needle in a haystack is that a strong enough magnet will pull the metal needle away from the straw that shelters it. The magnet attracts the metal. In this case I'm the magnet and the people we're looking for are the needle."

The guys thought about what Des said and they all started to smile as they understood what he was saying, some nodding.

But Slim wasn't sure if he liked the idea. "You mean instead of layin' low, you want to put yourself in the light, even more, to draw them out? You want to be bait?"

"Unless you have a better idea."

16

The Exchange

The morning dragged for Yarni after the unexpected visit from Rahllo. All she could do was sit at her desk and wonder how in the hell did two supposedly intelligent, beautiful young women go out for a night on the town dressed to kill and end up stealing a dope dealer's Cadillac Escalade filled with hot fur coats and enough heroin to put them both away for the rest of their natural lives.

Yarni shook her head. Each passing second Desember was proving to have more in common with Des than her chocolate, smooth skin, thick hair and engaging dark eyes.

Yarni thought the day couldn't perplex her any further until she got a call from her mother.

"I hate to call with only bad news," her mother said in an unsettling voice.

Yarni immediately thought the worst: the cancer was worse than the doctors first thought. *Why did shit like this happen to good people?* The only thing her mother had ever done in her life was try to help others. Yarni wasn't going to dwell upon why God had chosen this to be her mother's fate, but instead would be strong for Gloria.

"Don't be ridiculous, Ma. I'm always here for you, whenever and wherever you need me, good or bad. Now, what's up? What's going on? How are you feeling?" she asked, holding her breath.

"I think my husband is cheating on me," Gloria said bluntly. "Well, I know he is."

Yarni let out a sigh, relieved. Though, having cancer and also a husband having an affair is enough to kill a woman. Yarni couldn't ignore the pain in her mother's voice. "Why do you think that, Ma?"

Sam wasn't Yarni's father, but she knew how much Gloria loved the man. And up until that moment she thought Sam was a stand-up dude who had always been good to her mother. She'd never thought he'd do such a thing as cheat on Gloria. She'd always imagined that they'd live happily ever after. They always seemed so happy together. Maybe Gloria was mistaken? It had to be some kind of misunderstanding.

"Our CPA pointed out some unusual purchases on our credit card statement. I never go over that stuff," Gloria said. "And obviously Sam has been banking on me being a creature of habit."

"Maybe you're overreacting, Ma. Exactly what were the receipts for?" she asked.

"I'll fax them over so you can see them with your own eyes."

Gloria wasn't trying to hear it. "Yarni, I raised you! And I've been dealing with men since before you were born. Ask your father. Believe me, there isn't anything slow about yo' momma. I know what I know." Then she said, "That fool been renting a hotel room, twice a week, every week for the past six months. And even though we own a few restaurants, he's been gallivanting all around town wining and dining some woman." Gloria blew into the phone, displaying her frustration. "Don't get me started."

"How do you know all this, Ma?"

"Because I do. Now stop asking me silly questions."

Yarni's heart went out to her mother. A philandering husband was more than enough for the strongest woman in her right state of mind to deal with, but a woman with cancer?

Before she could respond, Layla buzzed her.

It was 2:30 on the dot, and Lava and Desember had arrived.

Yarni promised her mother she would call her right back.

The girls walked into her office. She looked the partners in crime up and down and then shook her head at the twosome. Desember wasn't wearing the outfit from last night.

Yarni was glad that Desember had at least taken a shower and guessed that she must have changed at Lava's house. "Have a seat," she ordered. "I'm about two minutes from hurting both of you."

"It's not what you think, Auntie," Lava said, trying to defuse the situation.

"Okay, let's see," retorted Yarni. "Did you," she pointed to Lava and Desember, "or did you not, jack a young fella's truck from a gas station?"

Desember cleared her throat. "Well, he shouldna stole the coat."

"I take that as a yes." Yarni looked out the window to the street. "Is the truck outside?"

Desember began to feel herself. "We might be young, but we ain't stupid."

"That's yet to be determined," Yarni countered. "Where is the vehicle?"

"We got it. He's just the kind of dude that can't really be trusted. He's a slickster and a lightweight prankster and sheister, so we wanted to make sure he has what he's supposed to deliver to us," Lava explained.

"It's called leverage," Desember chimed in.

Before Yarni could respond, Layla interrupted. "Mr. Bledsoe is here with his son."

Right on time. "Put them in the conference room, Layla. Tell them I'll be with them in a second, please." To the girls, she asked, "But the automobile is nearby?"

Desember nodded. "Yes, ma'am."

Yarni picked up her legal pad and hit them both upside the head as she walked out of her office with the girls in tow to make the exchange.

Once they entered the conference room, Yarni saw a grin spread across Rocko's face as he saw Desember. Yarni rolled her eyes at him, reached to take his hat off his head, "Have some re-spect. You are inside," and placed his Yankees cap on the table.

Rahllo said, "Let's get down to business."

Rocko stood up and removed the chinchilla from a brown

garment bag. "As good as new," he said with a smile, showing his white gold grill filled with diamonds.

Yarni could not believe her eyes. When she saw her chinchilla she almost went into convulsions. For a split second she was speechless.

"I'm sorry that I borrowed it," a contrite Desember said. "But this is why I missed my curfew; I refused to come back without it."

"She meant she wasn't going to come home without it," Lava seconded what Desember had stated.

"I swear, no disrespect was intended." Desember looked into Yarni's eyes, and when she saw the anger, she shifted her gaze to Rocko. She made him nervous. Good.

Yarni knew that Desember was wrong for taking her coat but that the girl meant well; still, this wasn't the time or place for her to discuss her thoughts about the situation with her.

Yarni said to Desember, "So now we have that all squared away and the coat is back in our possession, give these men the keys to their truck and disclose its location."

"There's just a little problem . . ."

"What?" Rahllo asked, beating his son to the punch.

"Well," Desember said, "you see, before I moved here I drove an Altima, so I wasn't really accustomed to driving no big SUV." Rahllo's and Rocko's eyes were glued on her.

"Man, don't tell me you hit something," Rocko speculated.

"I won't, then," she said seriously.

"You won't what?" Rahllo asked, trying to get some understanding of what Desember was trying to say.

"I won't tell you that I hit a light pole bending a corner and that since the truck was stolen, I left the sucker on the block of First and Federal Street."

"What?" This time it was Rahllo who was shocked.

"What in the hell was y'all doing over in the heart of Jackson Ward anyway?" Rahllo asked the girls. "That's no place for young ladies."

"Shorty, you gotta be crazy outta yo' rabbit-ass mind!" Rocko stood up.

Yarni said, "Desember, you left the car?" Yarni worried, trying to figure how she was going to defuse the situation.

Desember answered Rocko, "Just like you was crazy to run up in a got-damn club and steal some coats . . . my coat. You da one with some nerve."

"This shit is super serious." Rahllo was trying to keep his composure, but Yarni saw he was about to blow up.

Desember burst out laughing and threw Rocko the keys. "It's in the parking deck at the Coliseum. Here's the ticket. I was just pulling your leg, playboy."

Rocko looked like he couldn't help but dig Desember's style. He nodded. "It's all good."

"Now, I'd appreciate you'd stop running to your daddy and coming to my stepmother's job to straighten out the bullshit you start," Desember said.

Rocko and his father said at the same time, "This is your stepdaughter?"

"Yup." Though the test results hadn't officially come in yet, Yarni wasn't going to tell Rahllo any differently. Instead, she smiled and thought that Desember had a lot of spunk and heart to be only eighteen years old.

Rahllo caught Yarni giving Desember a look that said, "This ain't over."

"Yarni, don't be giving the girl no hard time when we leave. You know good and well you weren't no more of a saint than them when you were their age."

Desember asked, "What you mean?" seeming excited to hear a war story about Yarni.

Before they left, Desember asked Rocko what he planned to do with the other coats.

"They don't mean shit to me," he said. "I took 'em to disrespect the promoter. Why you ask?"

"Well, I would love to take them off of your hands. You could give them to me for a low price and I'll consider it a gesture of goodwill."

"A'ight, we gonna rap about it. I like you, you a little hustler."

"Natural born," Desember said.

"We have that in common, and just on the strength of you going out to breakfast, lunch or dinner with me, tomorrow I'll give 'em all to you to make up for the whole inconvenience."

"Deal." Desember shook his hand to seal the agreement, but her mind was on getting those coats and making money.

Yarni walked Rahllo and Rocko out. She told Desember, "Say your good-byes to your partner, because you're riding home with me."

Once in the car, Yarni didn't hold back her displeasure. "Girl, do you know you could have been locked up? Or killed? And you borrow my coat without even asking?"

The words went into one of Desember's ears and out the other. Her mind was still on the fact that she knew she could get rid of the coats in a matter of hours if she went back to Flowerville. And in the process, she would be able to see Fame.

Once they reached home, Desember got a call from Lava, making sure she had survived Yarni and Des's tongue lashings.

"I'm good." Desember asked Lava, "Will you go with me to North Carolina so I can dump the coats?"

"No doubt, I got ya. You don't even have to ask. But when you trying to go back?"

"ASAP!"

"Well, I can't go tomorrow because that's the anniversary for when Nasir was killed. I have to go to the cemetery first thing in the morning."

"OK, well after you go to the cemetery, or the next day."

"A'ight, I'm game."

17

Momma Don't Take
No Mess

It was a beautiful Saturday afternoon and after winning a couple games of Bingo, Joyce headed home three thousand dollars richer. The soulful voice of Marvin Gaye, her favorite singer, poured from the speakers as her Mercedes glided up Darbytown Road. The sophisticated S550 rode so smooth it barely needed her assistance—hell, with all the bells and whistles that came in these new cars, Joyce was convinced those German engineers could make the damn things drive by themselves if they wanted to. But until then, her seat belt was snug across her shoulder and waist, her hands on the wheel at ten and two. She couldn't operate half the gadgets the young folks thought they had to have now, but she knew how to get her car, a gift from her son, where she needed to go.

When Joyce pulled in front of her house she sensed something was out of order. After living in the same place for twenty-five years she could feel when things were awry. Or maybe, she thought to herself, she was just getting paranoid in her old age.

The neighbor's dog barked twice, probably at a bird or a cat, as she scooped up her purse and coat then exited the car before checking for something on the side of the house.

The moment she pulled her key from the front door lock and stepped into the foyer, the feeling from outside got stronger. It fact, it filled the house.

Six steps into the living room, her paranoia was upgraded to alarm when she heard a voice.

"'Bout time yo' old ass showed up."

Startled, but managing the urge to panic, Joyce faced the intruder.

The boy trespassing in her home was no more than eighteen. Wearing black denim from head to toe, black Nike boots and a black Yankees cap pulled low over his eyes.

"Don't make this any worse than it has to be, old lady. I'm just here to rough you up a little, take what I want and leave a message for your son." He spoke as casual as he would if he were running off a list of basic chores.

Until now, Joyce hadn't noticed the mess he'd made while rifling through her things. This pissed her off because she kept a clean, perfectly organized house. She bought nice things and hated when someone moved her stuff and didn't put it back in its place. Throw pillows and cushions from the sofa were tossed on the floor, a few picture frames were broken, and a half-eaten ham sandwich lay on her kitchen table.

The fucking nerve, Joyce thought, trying hard not to lose her composure. "Lil boy," she said, "I think you done made a mistake. Now, you need to get your lil narrow ass out of my gotdamn house while you still can."

The boy laughed. He seemed genuinely amused by her feistiness. "You funny," he said once he stopped chuckling. "But I ain't got time for yo' jokes. I got business to take care of."

He removed a small pistol from under his shirt and waved it at her. "You better go on ahead and sit yo' ass down while you still can, old lady," he looked into her eyes, "before I lay you down right here and now."

Joyce stood her ground. Matching his stare beat for beat, she didn't budge; she dropped her purse and jacket, though, which she'd been clutching to her body. Youngin's eyes grew big as saucers. "Make me, motherfucker," she said.

Where they'd been was now a six-shot Mossberg shotgun. As a precaution, Des always kept one hidden outside her house for her, just in case something didn't look right. Joyce had always argued that having that huge gun was both stupid and dangerous. But at the moment she was glad her son hadn't listened to her.

She lowered the short-barreled shotgun so it was aimed directly at the boy's groin. "Now, put that lil tiny thing away before I knock your dick in the dirt," she shot a slight smile at him, "lil boy."

Youngin sat the .32 down on the glass table by the sofa and put his hands where she could see them.

"Okay, now step your ass away from it and take yo' hat off in my got-damn house. Y'all young folks kill me with your so damn disrespectful." Joyce jerked the shotgun around as she spoke.

He removed his hat. As he put it down on the table, he

quickly picked up a vase and threw it at her to knock the gun out of her hand, but he didn't succeed. Instead, Joyce took the butt of the gun and with all her might cracked him as hard as she could upside the head, causing him to hit the floor face-first. Before the boy could recover from the blow she was standing on top of him.

"Turn over," she said with a kick in his side for emphasis.

"Okay, okay! Don't kill me!" The boy was stunned and had turned cowardly. She could tell that he had not only lost his gun but his bravado; he was damn right scared. And messing with Joyce, he should be. Getting on the woman's wrong side was nowhere anyone in their right mind wanted to be.

"Okay, okay, take it easy." He stumbled over his words. "I don't want no trouble, ma'am."

Just for the hell of it, Joyce booted him again, in the side. "I know you don't want no trouble now. But you were Billy-bad-ass a few seconds ago. Get yo' ass up." She didn't even care that he had blood trickling down the side of his head dropping on her freshly steam-cleaned carpet.

She got a better look at him. "I be got-damn, wait me a minute." She was surprised at what and who was standing in front of her. "You Beulah Pitchford's grandson, ain't cha?"

The boy obviously didn't know if he should tell the truth or lie. Lucky for him, he opted for the truth. "Yes, ma'am."

Ain't this a bitch, Joyce thought to herself. "Michelle's boy? Which boy you is—Michael or Melvin?"

He shook his head as if he was saying no, but answered, "I'm Michael," apparently too ashamed to look Joyce in the face.

For a second she was tempted to call the police on this fool, but Joyce was old school and came from a neighborhood that always took care of their own problems when they could. That's the way she was raised and that's the way she'd raised her children. "Get the fuck up and onto my couch. I'm calling your got-damn grandma. Coming in my motherfucking house trying to hurt me and break up my shit I done worked hard busting my ass for. Youngins with no got-damn respect for people or they shit. You better be lucky. I know Beulah and Michelle ain't bring you up like that."

He could barely move. Judging by the gash in his head, Joyce might have seriously hurt him, but she didn't care as she kicked him again as he was getting up.

"What's yo' grandmother's number? 'Cause I just can't believe this shit. You got the fucking nerve to be coming in my house, and I know yo' grandmother," she said, the shotgun in one hand and the phone in the other.

He muttered the number.

She dialed and Beulah picked up.

"Beulah, this is Joyce Taylor." Before Beulah could get her salutations out, Joyce said, "Yeah, I'm fucked-up now, 'bout to go to the penitentiary because I'm about to kill yo' got-damn grandson Michael. Don't you know that bastard done come in my house, trying to rob me, and do *God* knows what else to me."

Joyce was silent for a minute but never let the look of death she wore on her face stray from Michael's sight.

"Can you be here in fifteen minutes, because he got about twenty minutes left in this here life of his." Joyce said. Then asked, "You still drink scotch, don't you?"

Once she hung up the phone, she turned to Michael. "Yeah,

me and your grandma go waaayyy back." Joyce nodded. "I mean, way back. We done did some stuff together."

Michael looked scared and was still bleeding, but Joyce wasn't fazed by his blood at all.

"You got her two thousand dollars that she had under her mattress? 'Cause she said she ain't seen you since that got legs and walked up out of her house."

"I didn't take that."

"Boy, you getting high?" she asked, trying to figure out why he was doing such stupid things.

"No, ma'am," he said.

Joyce gave him another long look. "Who sent you here, child?"

He shrugged his shoulders.

"You don't know, or you ain't telling me?"

"I don't know."

Beulah was there in ten minutes flat. She came in and Joyce handed her a glass of scotch. Beulah was little and looked deceptively frail. She was close to eighty years old and had beautiful short silver hair and rich dark skin and she too looked good for her age. She went into her burgundy leather Aigner purse that had to be at least twenty years old and pulled out her .38 revolver and placed it on the bar, never acknowledging her grandson.

"Damn, you still toting?" Joyce asked.

"Yup. These young folks say they can't leave home without their American Express, but nowadays I can't leave home without my pistol. I ain't used it in a while but I've been itching to." Beulah took a sip of her scotch.

"I remember that night we was out at that house party and

you caught your first husband, Walter, with that huzzy and you shot him in the leg." Joyce laughed.

"He ain't walked right since and I heard his other leg ain't never been the same," Beulah said, and both ladies fell into laughter.

After Beulah had her second glass of scotch she walked over to Michael and slapped the taste out of his mouth. This was the first time either one of the women had even acknowledged him since his grandmother arrived. "You coming in Joyce's house, breaking up stuff, embarrassing me like you ain't got no home training. Negro, is you crazy?"

Michael wouldn't make eye contact with his grandmother.

"Look at me," she demanded.

Michael did as he was told.

"Who sent you here? You better tell me before this woman kills your ass and it ain't nothing none of us going to be able to do about it." She took another sip of her scotch, "And believe me, she will do it too and won't think nothing of it and will play a game of backgammon afterward."

"I can't tell you." He was shaking like a leaf.

"Why you can't?"

"You wanna die now or later?" Joyce asked as she lowered the gun to his torso, but his grandmother asked again, "Who sent you here? And don't lie to me, boy."

Beads of perspiration popped up on his top lip and forehead. "I can't tell you, because I don't know."

Beulah looked at Joyce and she cocked the gun.

"A guy just showed up at the Bill Robinson rec center and asked who wanted to make a quick four grand. He said all I had to do was scare Miss Joyce a lil bit, rough her up some, and break up some of her stuff. But I swear . . . I wasn't gon hurt ya."

Joyce knew damn well if she hadn't gotten the upper hand there's no telling what he would've done.

"You said you were given a message for my son." Joyce asked him, "What was it?"

Michael didn't say anything, his lip trembling.

Beulah went over to him and plucked his ear. "Spit it out— that's what you were paid to do, wasn't it?"

"Gimme the damn message," Joyce demanded.

Michael swallowed a lump in his throat. "Dude said to let your son know that nobody is off-limits."

18

Paying Respect

There'll be plenty of time to sleep once you're dead. The mantra was as familiar to Des as the color of his own eyes. A seasoned vet of the streets once said, "The cemetery is where a young hustla go to retire, and prison is where he goes to grow old."

Many women were left to fend for themselves because their men insisted on trying to beat the odds.

Nasir had been one of the growing numbers that fell prey to the streets. His father died when he was two and his mother put him out of the house at sixteen. His grandmother Joyce took him in her house, but Nasir took to hustling like a duck takes to water. Everybody and they momma told him he was just like his uncle Des. In his eyes it was the ultimate compliment—Des was a bona fide legend in the streets. Des's name still rang bells inside and outside the prison walls, even after doing a ten-year bid, and the fact he went down for another man's body when snitching was as in as fake hair and ass shots—but him keeping it real put him in the hood hall of fame.

Listening to one of his favorite Tupac cuts, Des sat in the front seat of his car wishing he could turn back the hands of time, wishing he would have never given Nasir his blessing to be a bigwig, to walk in his footsteps, when Des knew that the shoes were too complicated to fill. Des tried convincing himself that his nephew was already knee-deep in the game before Des had ever stepped foot out of prison, but what Nasir had been doing hadn't worked the way it should've. Nasir may have cracked the door to the dope game on his own, but with Des's connections and wisdom of the trade, the boy catapulted to heights beyond Des's wildest imagination. Heights that eventually cost him his life.

At the end of the song Des killed the engine and slid from the car carrying a bottle of Rémy—Nasir's favorite cognac—and a freshly rolled spliff as he made his way over to his nephew's grave. The soft grass, still wet from the earlier drizzle, held his footprints, marking a trail from his Bentley to the headstone. Des didn't believe in superstitions but he did believe in omens. Were the footprints trying to tell him something? Where was his own path headed?

Out of habit more than anything else he looked away from the impressions on the ground to survey the rest of his sur-roundings. Satisfied with seeing nothing but cold plots and warm flowers he turned his attention to the resting place of his nephew, unaware of the plots around him that were heating up.

"How's my favorite nephew?" he said, popping the cork on

the Rémy. He poured some on the ground, took a swallow for himself, and then placed the bottle with the remainder of the brown liquor on the stone. "Yarni keep telling me that you're in a better place, but I'm not sure if I buy it. A man makes his own Heaven—or Hell—right here while he's living, no matter how long or how short his time may be on Earth."

He removed a prerolled blunt from behind his ear. Des hadn't smoked weed in ten years before he and Slim lit one up during Nasir's repast. Since then, every time Des visited his nephew's grave he fired one up.

The pungent blue smoke curled under his nose before wafting through the air. A toke, holding his breath, eyes already beginning to redden . . . after he couldn't hold it any longer he exhaled.

"A lot of crazy shit going on, nephew," he said, returning to his one-sided monologue. "First, I get shot at by a mu'fucka that had to be at least two hundred yards away. Had to be some fucking sniper shit. Street niggas don't attack from two football fields away. They do drive-bys or kick in your door and start spraying automatic weapons, shit like that," Des mused.

One more hard pull on the blunt and his jaws collapsed like he was sucking on an extra-thick milkshake through a narrow straw. It relaxed him. Oh yeah, he was feeling it now.

"Two days later the church was robbed." Des hadn't started the ministry until after Nasir had passed. "I know you probably still having a hard time believing I'm running a multimillion-dollar cash flow through a megachurch. I struggle with it myself still, from time to time. But anyway, these fools put on a smoke-and-mirror act by running the pockets and purses of everybody attending the 12:30 service. Killed one of my partners—Tony—he was a good dude. You remember Tony, don't you?" Des nodded, thinking about the good memories for a second and then got back to what he was saying.

"I reimbursed every person there of their losses. No big deal. That shit was a bigger hit to my ego than my pocket. What's a few hundred thou amongst hustlers? Come to find out while the—what I didn't learn til afterward was a diversion—robbery was going on, them mu'fuckers had two more goons in the back forcing my treasurer to give them ten mil of my paper by pushing some fuckin' buttons on the computer."

Des shook his head. "Unbelievable, right? And no one's talking—that's even more un-fucking-believable. Not a peep. But best believe I'm gonna figure this shit out, though. That's why I stay ahead of the game . . . because I always figure it out. When I was sixteen and chumps that were getting lil money were putting rims on cars, I was buying houses and preparing for the storm that may come one day. Always prepare for the winter in the summer, ya know."

Speaking of the seasons reminded him. "Oh shit! I almost forgot. I got a eighteen-year-old daughter name Desember. She spells her name with an *s* instead of a *c,* though. I met her mother, Angie, back in the day at bike week and must've left more than a lasting impression. We waiting on the DNA, but the girl resemble me so much it's a no-brainer. Yarni ain't really feeling it. I can see it in her eyes, but she trying to stay cool about it. It ain't the girl's fault. Really, ain't anybody's fault. But that don't make shit any easier. I wish you were here to meet her. She seems real cool. She and Lava—your other half—hit it right off."

When his pocket vibrated, he fumbled for his phone.

"What up, Ma? I'm at the cemetery, venting with Nasir."

Joyce told him about the botched home invasion, but she assured him that it was all under control.

"I'll be right there." He hung up. He poured the rest of the cognac out. "I gotta cut this one short, nephew. The shit just won't stop."

19

On Stomping Ground

True to his word, Rocko came through with the furs his crew had jacked from Scrooge's party. Fifty-six in all.

Rocko and Desember negotiated his take from the sale of the furs. He suggested twenty percent. "Or whatever you think is fair," he said.

Desember wanted to further extend the olive branch and decided his offer was more than fair.

"You got a deal," Desember agreed, and smiled.

That was all Desember needed to push her back to her stomping ground. She couldn't wait to set foot back in North Carolina. The anticipation of the few stacks she expected to get from the coats excited her, but more than anything, the opportunity to see her man had her amped.

As she made plans to put the trip in motion, nobody back

home—not Fame or anyone else—had any idea she was coming. She didn't even come clean to Yarni and Des. She felt bad about not telling them but she didn't want to risk them vetoing the trip.

That wasn't a chance Desember was willing to take.

$ $ $

Three days later, Lava and Desember were on the road. Lava drove most of the way until they got into the city, then Desember took the wheel. She was back on her home soil, yet it felt sort of weird. Like she'd been gone for a year instead of just two weeks. She set up shop in the apartment of her best friend, Kayla, and let her clientele flock to her. And once she started selling the coats, it was like riding a bike; six hours later, all but four of the coats were sold.

As she watched Desember count her money, barely keeping a hold of the huge stack of bills, Lava said, impressed, "Damn girl, you the man down this bitch."

"Girl, you ain't know I was the shit when it came to moving any and everything? I just have to figure out a way to implement my hustle up there in Richmond."

"I'm sure you will," Lava assured her.

They wrapped up things at Kayla's apartment and headed to Desember's mother's house. Desember wanted to grab a few things and be in and out of there before her mother, Angie, got home from work.

Desember searched through a dresser drawer in her old room and found a gold heart-shaped locket.

"Fame gave this to me for my birthday." Desember opened the locket and showed Lava the picture she and Fame had taken at a Young Jeezy concert, their smiling faces filling the small opening in the locket.

Desember stared at the photo and was so engrossed by memories that she didn't hear someone messing with the front door.

"I think someone's at the door," Lava said in a low tone. "I thought you said your mother and stepdad were at work." Desember had already shared with her why Fame and her mother had all but forced her to leave town: after Fame was nearly killed by gunfire, they didn't think North Carolina was safe for her. No one was sure if Fame was indeed the real target. Also Fame feared his family might suspect that Desember set him up and try to get revenge. Their relationship was both passionate and volatile, and they had just reconciled before he was shot.

Desember jerked her head up, her eyes open wide. "They are."

That's all Lava needed to hear. She eased the chrome nine, one of two Nasir had given her, from her purse. "Just in case," she said almost in a whisper.

They heard footsteps coming closer to the bedroom.

The two looked at each other. Desember shrugged her shoulders in confusion.

Then a voice: "Who's in there?"

Desember sighed in relief. It was her mother.

"It's me, Ma."

Lava dropped the nine back in her purse as Angie opened the door. "You trying to scare me to death, girl? What are you doing here?"

"I do live here." Desember frowned. "Or do I?"

Angie and Desember hadn't been tight since Angie married Joe. As far as Desember was concerned, he was an abusive womanizer and a first-class jerk who drank too much. She hated that her mother would accept the shit he dished out. He was the wedge that pushed the mother and daughter apart, in heart and distance, causing Desember to swear that she would never depend on a man for her livelihood.

"Don't be smart. As long as I have a place to lay my head, you will too." Angie noticed Lava for the first time chilling in the corner. "Who's your friend?"

"This is my cousin, Lava." Lava, sensing they needed a moment alone, said, "If you don't mind, I gotta get something from the car."

Mother and daughter quietly stared at each other for a few moments. Angie was the first to burst the bubble of silence surrounding them.

"How do you feel now that you've finally met your father?"

The little girl inside of Desember wanted to scream out, "He's everything I ever wanted!" But instead she said, "I won't know how I feel until the DNA results come back."

Angie's facial features sank a little. "I know I haven't been completely honest with you in the past, Desember, but you have my word." Angie looked in Desember's eyes. "Des is your father. I knew the moment I conceived. This isn't any bullshit this time."

If Desember looked deep enough into her mother's eyes, she would see that Angie never stopped loving Des. "Well, only time will tell," she said, nonchalantly. Angie had lied about who Desember's father was so many times that Desember refused to get her hopes up.

Angie asked, "What's his wife like?"

Desember thought about the question, and for the first time, her real impression of Yarni came to mind. "I'll make a deal with you," she said to her mother. "You tell me about how you and Des met back in the day and I'll tell you about Yarni, Des's wife."

20

Family Jewels

Yarni walked past Desember's room and heard a surprising noise coming from the other side of the door. She listened for a second and then she knocked. "Desember?" When the girl didn't answer, she called out again, "Desember?" After the second time, Yarni let herself into the room. "Honey, are you okay?"

Desember, laying flat on her stomach with her face buried in a pillow, was in tears. "What's wrong?" Yarni asked.

"Nothing." Desember raised her head and tried to wipe away her tears but they would not stop falling down her face.

"Well, 'nothing' doesn't cause tears to fall from your eyes uncontrollably, Dee. So tell the B.S. to someone else, not me. We agreed just the other day at my office that we would not bullshit each other, right?" Yarni sincerely wanted to help. Instinctively, like a mother.

She'd made Desember laugh a little. "You wouldn't understand."

"You ought to be convinced by now that I was your age before. And I know it sounds cliché, but everything that you did I've already done." Yarni looked at Desember and handed her a tissue. "I made a lot of mistakes growing up too, but from each and every one of them I was able to gather a wealth of information about men, women, life and bullshit in general. Maybe if you let me, I can pass on what I learned." Yarni took a deep breath. "And who knows, maybe I can learn a thing or two from you too."

Desember blew her nose, then with another tissue she wiped away her tears. After, she took a deep breath and looked up at Yarni. "Have you ever loved someone so much that you'd risk your life for theirs?"

"Very much so. I married him."

A few seconds passed as Yarni waited quietly for Desember to continue.

"Please don't be mad at me, but I snuck down to North Carolina to see Fame."

"I'm not going to fuss, but you do understand that you can't go back there. It's just not safe, Dee."

"Well, you don't have to worry because I'm not welcome there anymore," Desember said, blowing her nose and starting to cry again. "He told me that he robbed the wrong person and it's just a matter of time before . . ." The tears were coming so fast now that she couldn't get the words out, "before . . ." Desember couldn't speak through her sobs.

"Take a deep breath; it's going to be okay," Yarni said in a calm, loving tone. She put her arms around Desember. "Deep breath. Come on now, inhale. Another deep breath."

Desember inhaled and exhaled a few times as Yarni directed and then started speaking again. "He said it's only a matter of time before they kill him. And that I need to go on with my life and . . ." She started to sob harder as the words came out, ". . . to forget I ever knew him. It's almost like the words he said to me were daggers."

"I know. I've been there before," Yarni said as she embraced Desember tighter.

"For him to know I love him the way I do and to tell me to get out of his life? I felt like I wanted to just die, like . . . like I was living that Lauryn Hill song, like he was killing me softly."

"Yes, I know, baby," Yarni said with an understanding heart. "Honestly, I faced a very similar situation when Des went to jail."

"Really?" Desember asked. Hearing stories about Des intrigued her, even though she was feeling down at the moment.

Yarni didn't hold back. "I was just about around your age, I guess, and he was my world. I had abandoned my mother and my friends, and once he was sentenced I was left to fend for myself. Because he had so much time, he told me to move on with my life and not wait for him. I felt so betrayed by him. The system had already hurt me by putting him in jail and then he was being so cold and callous toward me. I wanted to know how he could tell me something like that."

"That's how Fame is acting toward me. He told me to forget all about him. Act like I never knew him. I don't understand how he could love me so much one day, and then the next week, he shuts the door in my face. And wants me to walk away."

"But love isn't like a faucet: you can't turn it off and on."

"You got that right."

"How could you do that when he's been your world, right?"

"Yup. You do understand where I'm coming from." Desember realized that she and Yarni had more in common than she'd thought.

"Nobody ever tells us when we get involved with so-called bad guys about the real dangers, the heartaches and pains that come with being a hustler's wife."

Twisting her face, Desember told Yarni that Fame never sold drugs.

"Hustling comes in many forms, Dee. The fundamental differences are if they are legal or illegal: at the end of day, it's all about getting a dollar."

"You are right," Desember agreed.

"People always say don't get involved with those guys, but nobody ever gives you the real-deal orientation for dealing with them. The bottom line is, we can't control who we fall in love with. But we absolutely must be aware of the pitfalls and perils that come with being with a street dude. You could get kidnapped or caught up in a case with them or even lose your freedom or your life just for being associated—not to mention the toll it takes on your heart, soul, mind, spirit and sanity. It's like gambling sometimes: high risk, high reward."

Desember listened attentively, not interrupting.

Yarni looked in Desember's eyes as she continued, "Nothing

can really prepare you for the B.S. that comes with life in general, but for street life—there should probably be some kind of mandatory orientation or guide for being a hustler's wife and dealing with the other women, the jealous people, the police, the greed. All of it is a cancer." She went on, "The heartaches and heartbreaks of a hustler's wife can drive you into the crack house or the crazy house, because only the strong can survive. When we deal with these guys, we have to know that this is what comes with the game."

Desember digested all that Yarni said. It made her look at things in her life in a totally different light. Desember's wheels were turning in her head. "Wow! That was powerful food for thought. But why do we gamble with our lives?" she asked.

"In life, nothing is free. Eventually you have to pay the piper." Yarni paused for a second, thinking how the same thing applied to Des's life. He had done things and now they seemed to be chasing him.

"Dee, I know it hurts, but you should be glad that Fame loves you enough to protect you. Some men are so selfish that they will let you die right beside them on some fake Bonnie and Clyde type stuff."

They both were quiet when Des entered the room. "What's going on in here? You girls bonding?" he asked.

"Yup, I'm finding out that Yarni isn't the wicked stepmother after all," Desember said, smiling. "She's giving me priceless heirlooms of wisdom."

"Oh so she's your stepmother now?" he questioned.

"A figure of speech," Desember countered.

Yarni put her arm around Desember's shoulder, drawing her

close. "You know, it doesn't really matter what the test says. In my heart you are my baby, and even though we weren't connected by the umbilical cord, we are connected by heart, and as far as I'm concerned you're my daughter too."

Desember gave Yarni a hug. "That made my day. I'm not usually no crybaby, but you making me cry again."

"I mean it." Yarni looked into Desember's eyes and knew in her heart that Desember was Des's daughter, without a doubt.

"Well, look what the mailman brought." Des held up the envelope. "Do we even want to know?" he asked. Desember grabbed for it but he pulled it out of her reach. "I mean, we all seem to be getting along as one big happy family."

"Yes, regardless of what the test says, I believe you belong here with us," Yarni said, half joking. "But the next time you need to borrow something out of my closet just make sure you ask first."

Desember agreed, but her focus was on Des, trying to get the valuable information he was holding hostage. She was shaking inside. And she didn't know if it was because Des might not be her real father, or because he may be.

Des tortured the two ladies for a few more moments before opening the results, and when he did, in a Maury Povich voice he said, "I'm the father."

Desember started dancing around. "So I guess you got a lot of making up to do, huh, Dad?"

The moment was surreal. They had all known there was a high probability that this day would come, but the reality was enormous.

Yarni had thought she'd lose part of her intimacy with her husband; instead, she'd gained a second daughter . . . and a friend.

Life would never be the same for Desember. From the only child of a single parent to a big sister, a Daddy's girl with two moms—winning the lottery wouldn't have made her feel as excited and happy as she was now. Well, maybe just as happy.

"After things calm down here, I'm going to have my sister throw you a welcome to the family party!"

Des smiled because he knew that Yarni was adjusting to the idea that Desember was now officially a part of their lives. He took it all in. He loved nothing in the world more than family. Love is family, and family is love.

21

How Dare He?

After the positive results from the DNA test came in, Des, Yarni, Desi, Desember and Joyce all went out to a posh restaurant for a celebratory dinner. Little Desi had a ball, but she couldn't figure out what all the fuss was about. She already knew Desember was her big sister; they even resembled each other. Grown-ups can make things so complicated at times, she thought.

The next few days breezed by without incident, which was a welcome change from the prior week.

Des was still extra-cautious and made sure the whole family—including Joyce—let him know where they were going to be at all times. Until the identity of the person or persons responsible for the shooting and robbery were discovered, that's the way it had to be.

Joyce had been the hardest to convince to stick to the script.

"I'm a grown-ass, unmarried woman," she protested loud and clear. "And my days of reporting my comings and goings to a man are over."

Des figured she didn't want him to know how often she frequented the bingo spot. At least that's where she said she went every Monday, Wednesday, Friday and more often than not, Saturday evenings. Maybe she had a male friend she was keeping a secret, Des wondered. Before leaving the restaurant to head home, Des told his mother, firmly, that it had to be this way until he got to the bottom of things.

$ $ $

Later that night, after the celebration, it didn't take long for Des and Yarni to get busy.

Yarni's breathing became quicker and quicker. "Don't." Short breath. "Stop," she managed to get out. Des had been making love to her for an hour.

The soft sheets, tangled around one of her raised legs shimmied with each and every one of Des's deep thrusts.

They were in perfect harmony, like hearing a favorite song at just the right moment. Magical.

Desi had been long put to bed. Yarni tried to keep the volume of her cries of bliss to a minimum in order not to wake her.

Then he hit the spot.

"Oh-my-God!" She shouted, forgetting all about the noise. "Please . . . Des . . . don't make me . . . come," she cried, matching his rhythm.

Then she shook.

Des knew the sign.

He had taken her to her limit; and it was a good thing too, because he'd reached his own.

Now he pushed himself inside her as far as he could go.

They stayed that way for a few beats. Then they clammed together.

After a couple of minutes of heavy panting, unable to distinquish where hers began and his stopped, Des finally spoke.

"I love you."

"I love you too, Des."

Their bodies were painted with perspiration and their breathing was just beginning to become normal. As normal as it gets for two people in love, lying almost on top of each other in the clothes they were born with.

"What time does your flight leave tomorrow?" he asked.

She could still smell the sliced peaches they'd had so much fun with on his breath.

"At three," she said. "I'm supposed to arrive in Florida at six-thirty. You sure you don't want to come with me?"

Her mother's operation was scheduled to be performed the following morning after Yarni's arrival. She planned to stay with her mother until she recovered from surgery. "The doctors say she'll be in the hospital for a couple of days before she can be released."

Des turned on his back, looking at the ceiling. "Of course I want to go with you to be there for Gloria. But I can't," he said. "There's too much going on."

Yarni understood. She knew how much he loved Gloria. He

was doing what he thought was best. He had to stay and hold down the fort.

$ $ $

Gloria and her husband, Sam, were waiting by a Starbucks when Yarni finally deplaned and headed for baggage claim.

"Mommeee!" Yarni ran across the carpeted corridor and gave her mother a huge hug.

"Girl," Gloria spoke in a hushed voice still in Yarni's embrace, "people are staring at us. You acting like a little girl," she added.

"I don't care who is looking. And I am, and always will be, your little girl! At least that's what you used to tell me, anyway." Yarni finally let her mother go. "I'm starved," she added. "I hope y'all haven't eaten."

"Hey, Sam," Yarni spoke to her stepfather but offered him no embrace. That was the closest she came to even acknowledging him. Ever since her mother told her about the indecent extracurricular activities she suspected him of, Yarni felt differently about the man.

On the way to the baggage claim Sam asked, "How was your flight?"

The flight was the worst. Yarni vowed never to fly coach again. She had been penned in a middle seat between an old man who smelled like Ben-Gay and Old Spice, and a mother with a baby that wouldn't stop crying or hitting her. Between the noise, the spats and the horrible scent, her head wouldn't stop throbbing. She thought the madness would never end.

She kept her response short and blunt. "Just glad to be here."

Sam was either too dumb to realize she was giving him the cold shoulder or too big-headed to care. No sweat off her back either way.

After they got Yarni's two oversized pieces of Louis Vuitton luggage secured in the SUV, Gloria suggested they go to a place she knew that perfectly grilled steaks.

They ate outside under a canopy, and Yarni could hardly believe how wonderful the weather was: eighty degrees in December. "They say we may get a few dustings of snow back home."

"That's just one of the reasons you should consider moving down here." Gloria had been trying to convince her and Des to move to Florida for years.

It was tempting, Yarni thought to herself. She could practice law anywhere.

"Maybe we will. One day," Yarni mused.

Sam was on his fourth drink and paying the girls no mind. Yarni didn't care in the least, but she felt sad for her mother.

The next morning, Yarni and her mother headed to the hospital for Gloria's lumpectomy. As Gloria lay in the back of the building somewhere getting prepped for her surgery, there were two questions that Yarni could not get out of her head: where in the hell was Gloria's husband, Sam, and more importantly, why was he not at her mother's side? It was killing her that Sam had not been home since the night before. Both Sam and her mother had picked Yarni up from the airport and took her to dinner. Then Yarni and Gloria decided to go to Target, and when they returned Sam was nowhere to be found.

"Ma, do you think that Sam will meet us?" she asked on the way to the hospital.

"I don't know. I called him and he didn't answer. Maybe he's out with one of his skallywags." She sucked her teeth. "But, I tell you what, I can't focus on him now; I have to give my all to myself and getting me better."

Yarni agreed. "That's right, Mommy, you sure do!"

Gloria sighed. "Oh honey, once I'm back, trust and believe I will deal with him, because he's been getting out of control. Don't you worry, he will be dealt with. It just takes too much of my energy right now."

Yarni didn't comment because she didn't want to get her mother worked up. Yarni always knew her mother to be a strong woman who normally would never put up with any kind of nonsense from a man, not even a husband.

Once Gloria was wheeled off for surgery, time flew as Yarni began on some of the work that she had brought with her. She was sitting in the waiting room when someone startled her. "Hey, pretty lady."

Yarni looked up and was surprised to see her father, Lloyd. "Dang, Daddy, what are you doing here?"

He leaned down to kiss her on the cheek. "I decided at the last minute to get on the first flight out this morning. I had been kicking around the idea since you told me about your mother. She was my good friend and wife for many years, mother of my child, and she was there for me all that time I was in prison, so the least I can do is come visit her when she needs her loved ones around her the most."

Yarni looked at her father as he stood with his hands in the pockets of his slacks. Lloyd was so slick and his swagger was still swift. It was almost like he didn't walk, he glided across the floor. And though he was well over fifty years old, he hadn't lost his charm, charisma or quick wit. With his salt-and-pepper hair, he was still very handsome and debonair; she could tell why her mother had loved him for so many years.

"That's big of you, Daddy. But I thought you were going to hang around Richmond in case Des needs help with things."

He shooed off that thought. "Des got Joyce, plus your nanny; Desember and Bambi around there to help out too. And he has Stanka and Slim watching his back. But I asked myself, who do you have here with you? So Big Daddy is here to the rescue." He took the seat beside her.

"Thank you, Daddy." She smiled.

"I know it's got to be tough on you, baby, dealing with all this shitty bullshit. From those ungrateful ass shucking and jiving clients of yours, and then Des's situation, the wild-buck step-daughter and Joyce . . . " He shook his head. "That lady is something else."

"Ain't she?" Yarni agreed. "I think she means well, but she's just misunderstood."

Yarni thought about when Des first went to jail. She was a week away from her eighteenth birthday, and Des had been her knight in shining armor. She was devastated when the judge banged his gavel and ordered the man she loved more than life itself to what might as well have been an eternity.

When Yarni finally got back to the condo that she and Des shared, the place was empty. Joyce had hired movers to take everything. Clothes. Jewelry. Furniture. Everything. At that time, Joyce thought that Yarni was a young gold-digging chick looking for a free ride from her son. It took years before Joyce realized how much Yarni really loved Des.

Yarni shared that story with her father.

"That was some bullshit," her father stated.

"Yeah, it was, but she was looking out for the best interests of her son. She really does love him after all."

"You might be right, but she's still a piece of work. Anyway, I wanted to be here for Gloria and for you also. So how you holding up with everything going on?"

Yarni took a deep breath. "You mean dealing with Mom's situation?"

"No," he shook his head, "not just that. The church, Des, Desember, work—everything."

"It's all wearing on me for real. Desember coming to live with us, work, all of Des's bullshit, raising a child."

Lloyd put his arms around her to comfort her. And when she felt the embrace from her father, she felt comforted, protected, and she let loose her tears.

"Ahh, baby, just let it out." He reached for his handkerchief.

"Oh, Daddy, I don't know what to do. Just seems like I have the weight of the world on my shoulders," she managed to get out between sobs.

"I can imagine. You know I love Des like a son, but if it gets to be too much for you, you know you can step away if you need to."

"Yeah, but that's not really an option."

"I know, but sometimes you have to do what's right for you."

"Daddy, I only want Des to decide what it is that he wants,

get his act together, and keep both feet in a legitimate business. I just feel that we've strived so much to get to where we are and now it all may be taken away because he won't stop indulging in that life and because of things he did in his past."

"That's understandable, but remember who you married," her father said. Before she could respond, her phone rang. It was Layla giving her the good news that Tangaleena's case had been null processed. Yarni didn't know which she was happier about: the news that she received on her client or the fact that Layla's call got her out of the long lecture Lloyd was about to give her that she needed to hear but didn't want to listen to.

Actually, Yarni had lied to her father. She had thought about leaving Des almost every time she stepped foot inside a courtroom. Whenever she heard a judge sentence another black man to a life behind bars she remembered how she used to think when she was young that being the girlfriend or wife of one of the most feared and respected hustlers in the city was exciting.

Invidious.

She wanted more.

Needed more.

Deserved more.

Leaving Des would be one of the hardest things she'd ever done, but things in their life seemed to get only more complicated throughout the years. But the love they shared seemed to keep them together.

The following evening after Yarni got Gloria home and settled, Gloria slept while Yarni and Lloyd played Scrabble, and her father asked, "Where is the joker she married?"

"I was wondering the same thing."

It was burning Yarni up that Sam had not even called to check on Gloria. Once the game was over, Yarni got Lloyd set up in one of the guest rooms and went into her own room and pulled out the papers Gloria had faxed her. When Gloria first mentioned her problems with Sam, Yarni had hired a private investigator. She looked at the charges on the bill and the report the detective had given her to figure out the places that Sam frequented and compared it to a calendar. Today was Tuesday and on every Tuesday, the dummy usually dined at the same restaurant.

She knocked on the door to the guest bedroom. "Daddy, listen out for Ma for me, please. I gotta make a quick run."

She knew that she shouldn't stick her nose in other people's business, but this was her mother and Yarni couldn't help it. She grabbed the keys to Gloria's car and headed down to the restaurant.

She pulled the luxury vehicle in front and tipped the valet to keep it there. "I'll only be a few minutes," she said with a smile. Inside was upscale but most of the patrons were casually dressed.

"Ma'am, do you have a reservation?" the maître d' asked after he greeted her.

"I'm looking for my stepfather. I believe he's here, seated already," she said with a grin. Yarni scanned the restaurant, and spotted Sam sitting in the company of a woman with whom he was laughing, having a grand old time. Yarni's blood began to boil. *The damn gall of him.* She strolled across the dining room with rage in her eyes.

By the time Sam saw her, she was conveniently and swiftly

placing her bag on the back of a chair as she took a seat at their table. "Hi, Sam," she said. "Well, aren't you going to introduce me?" Sam seemed to be too busy picking up his smile off the floor and was at a loss for words, so Yarni kept talking. "Hi." With a warm smile, she extended her hand to the woman sitting there. "I'm Yarnise, and you are . . . ?"

"Cheryl." The lady, who had a short savvy haircut and was smoking a long skinny cigarette, clasped Yarni's hand in return, but by the look on her face, she was confused about what was going on.

The waitress came over. "Would you like something?"

Sam finally managed to speak. "No, she's not staying."

"I would." Yarni smiled at the waitress. "I will have a Belvedere with cranberry juice, please." She then looked at Sam. "How do you think I should handle this? I can—"

"Handle what? Sam?" Cheryl looked at him for an explanation. Sam, who was usually dapper, smooth and quick on his feet, obviously could not figure out how to play this. He'd experienced firsthand how Yarni was in her younger days, and he didn't want to draw attention to the table.

"So what now?" Sam asked Yarni in a low tone.

"Sam?" Cheryl was in a state of shock, not knowing what was going on or what to do.

Yarni smirked and put her finger up and spoke at a level just above a whisper, but loud enough for both Cheryl and Sam to hear her. "I got you, Cheryl. I promise I do. Just hold tight, because you seem like a nice enough lady. I'm not going to hold his bullshit against you. I'm going to fill you in, in a minute."

Just then the waitress placed Yarni's drink in front of her.

"You know, Sam, after I finish this drink, I'm going to let you know how we going to proceed."

"Proceed with what?" Cheryl asked.

"You see, Cheryl, I'm his stepdaughter, which means he's married to my mother. My mother, who was recently diagnosed with breast cancer. This is the same woman just released from the hospital after undergoing a lumpectomy just a little over . . ." Yarni looked at her Chopard watch, ". . . four hours ago." Cheryl looked mortified, but that didn't faze Yarni in the least; she kept going. "And her thoughtful husband did not have the love, respect or common courtesy to even come to the hospital and see about his wife—who, like I said, happens to be my mother." Yarni was as cool as the cat on the Cheetos commercial as she said this, then took a sip of her drink.

"Oh my God," Cheryl said.

Yarni turned to look at Sam. "See, you might not care about your wife, but I care about my mother."

"Please, I didn't know. Let me apologize," Cheryl said. "Damn, Sam, I would have never suspected you to be that kind of man."

Yarni took a sip of her drink, then said, "If he treats his wife like that, the one he stood in front of not only his friends and family but God and said I do to, imagine how he'd treat you."

Cheryl shook her head. "You are something else, Sam. You told me your wife was an alcoholic and in rehab."

"Guess what, Cheryl? He lied," Yarni said sweetly.

Cheryl stood up. "Lose my number," she pointed at Sam. "Do me a favor and delete it please."

"Good move, girl," Yarni said as Cheryl reached for her purse before rolling out.

Yarni gulped down the last of her drink. "Now, here's what you're going to do," she said to Sam.

"What's that?" Sam asked, still in a state of disbelief that everything had unraveled so quickly.

"You are going to run home to your sick wife, who needs plenty of rest and can't drive or do any strenuous exercises." She spoke slowly and clearly so he wouldn't miss a beat. "And you are going to be at her beck and call and cater to every one of her needs, big or small, hand and foot, never leaving her side." She put up her index finger. "Not one complaint, frown or fit for the next three weeks, and then again for the six weeks of her radiation treatments. Do not spend one dime of my mother's money on any of your 'friends'—or yourself, for that matter."

"I don't spend your mother's money. I work for mine."

"We are not going to go there," Yarni said before continuing with the instructions. "Once the radiation treatments are complete, you are going to wait a few weeks, after which time you will go quietly and file for a divorce, not asking for a got-damn iron dime of my mother's money. You will make this as peaceful as absolutely fucking possible." Yarni never broke eye contact with Sam. "And Sam"—she stood up—"please don't fuck with me, because you know my history and my pedigree. And I don't fucking play when it comes to my mother."

22

Big Balls

It was Yarni's first day back in her office after her weeklong visit with her mother. She hated to leave Gloria's side, but she had to get back to Desi and to work. However, she did have something to look forward to: the date night Des had promised her. With all the mayhem and confusion of late, the couple had had precious little alone time to focus on their relationship and each other. Yarni understood that things were hectic but she desperately missed the quality time that she and Des always had had together—until now.

"You have a Mr. Cook'em-up here to see you."

"Cook'em-up?" Yarni questioned.

Though she had only been in the man's company a couple of times, she had heard plenty of dirt about him from Bambi, who couldn't stand him. Bambi swore Cook'em-up couldn't be trusted, even though his undying loyalty for her husband, Lynx, and

Lynx's brother, C-Note, should have made her feel differently. Cook'em-up and Lynx went way back and were as thick as thieves. However, his name stayed ringing bells in the streets, because he was a known hit man who considered nobody off-limits. After all the people he'd killed, nobody in the city understood how he had stayed out on the streets for so long without being arrested.

"He says it's urgent and will only take a few minutes of your time. He says he knows how valuable your 'mu'fucking time' is," Layla said with a slight chuckle.

What could this dude possibly want? Had he finally been arrested for a murder? Yarni wondered. *Had someone actually dropped a dime on him? Were the ghosts from his past catching up with him?* Yarni's curiosity was killing her; she wondered what he'd done and how he'd managed to get caught.

"Show him in," Yarni told Layla, and then, "And by the way, any word on those phone records?" They had been waiting for the phone records from Roxanne's cell phone for a couple of weeks.

"Yes, we will have the name of the caller and the billing address for the phone within seventy-two hours. Trust me, I'm on it. Do you want Mr. Cook'em-up in the conference room or your office?"

"In here is fine."

Cook'em-up strolled through the door of Yarni's posh office. "So, how are you, Cook'em-up?" She stood to offer him a seat. She felt like a dwarf to his 6'5" tall, thin frame. He looked like he could be a retired basketball player, not a hit man.

"Fair, but the sun going to be shining for me real soon," he said to her as he looked at the photos of Yarni and her family that were displayed on the shelves in her office.

"How can I help you?"

He ignored her as he continued to admire photos of the many memories displayed around the room. "That dude clean up real good, don't he?" he asked, looking at her and Des's wedding photo. They were married when the new millennium came in and 1999 left, in Vegas at the Paris hotel atop the Eiffel Tower.

"He does."

Cook'em-up took off his Ray-Ban sunglasses and shook his head. "That nigga got it made. He has everything. The world is at his feet. Always did have plenty of exotic women and money gravitating to him." Cook'em-up shook his head like he knew something that Yarni didn't.

Bambi had told her that the man could be a bona fide hater, so she ignored his comments about the women.

"So how's business going?" he asked, moving to study all her achievements on the wall.

"Business is good. Steady. No complaints. My colleagues thought it would get a little busier with the recession and all, that crime would pay, but to everyone's surprise it hasn't gotten crazy busy," Yarni said, with a growing bad feeling in her gut.

"Do you give incentives for referrals?"

"My rates are always fair regardless of how I get my clients," Yarni said, "but you are like family, so I would definitely give you the absolute rock-bottom price."

The way Cook'em-up walked around her office like he owned the place would have intimidated most, but Yarni had been dealing with guys like him since her late teens. She had shared her bed with a couple, and later went on to represent guys like him in a courtroom.

"Really?" he asked.

"You know that. But that isn't why you're here," she stated.

"I sent you my cousin and he was grateful for the job you did. He said you worth every penny," Cook'em-up said, finally taking the seat that she had offered him five minutes ago.

"Who's your cousin?" Yarni asked. She was growing impatient and wanted to know what in the hell he was really there for and wished he'd get to his point. Time was money and he didn't seem to be spending any, only wasting hers.

"Douglas Crumb, but everybody calls him Bug." He searched her face for fear or surprise, but there was none to be found. "You know, the nigga you shot, back in the day? On Grace Street?"

Chills went up Yarni's spine but she didn't let on. She had her poker face on. This was the day that she had been dreading. Her worst dream was becoming reality . . . a ghost from her wild past had finally resurfaced.

"I don't know what you're talking about." She followed the advice that she gave to her clients: never confess to anything.

"Oh you know. You know good and well," he said with confidence. She saw the confusion on his face when he realized she wasn't biting.

"See, Bug doesn't remember you, but I do." Cook'em-up laughed as he put his feet up on Yarni's desk.

"Please remove your feet from my desk." She stood, her arms folded.

Cook'em-up ignored her request, looked into her eyes, and kept talking. "That nigga done a lot of fucked-up shit," he nodded, "when he wasn't in his right state of mind." He put up a finger. "But after getting with dat bitch of his, the nigga finally got himself all the way together. Nevertheless the fact still remains, too many years of getting high can really fuck a nigga up for life." Cook'em-up shook his head. "He can't remember shit. But me?" He pointed to his chest. "I ain't never got high. I always loved money and seek out every opportunity to get it. So, me? I remember everything. Never forget a face or name."

"Cook'em-up, this doesn't have anything to do with me. I think you are sadly mistaken. And I'm going to ask you one more time to get your feet off my desk."

He continued, not moving. "I was the driver of the van. I started to get out and gun yo' ass down," he admitted, "but I respected your gangsta. Was sure that we'd meet again, but our paths separated and who'd ever thought you'd go on and be a renowned lawyer and me one of the best hit men to ever walk these streets." He finally set his feet down.

"You're out of your mind. You said you don't do drugs, but you must have been smoking something," Yarni stated.

Cook'em-up paused, and she knew he was second-guessing himself about whether it was her or not.

"Yo, this is what it is." He reestablished eye contact with her and said, "You need to let your husband know that this shit is not a fucking game. He ain't getting the picture. He's going to die a slow painful death, but not before I take everything from him."

Yarni was stunned and before she could gather her thoughts and speak, he continued, "I'm talking about fucking with and destroying everybody who means something to dat nigga. I'm going to make sure he's broke and then I'm going to take his freedom, and when he's in the pen I'll make sure he dies a slow, painful death."

"You are such a big man, why don't you tell him yourself?" Yarni asked, forcing herself to keep her voice steady. She wasn't going to give Cook'em-up the satisfaction of seeing any fear in her eyes. "As a matter of fact, you need to leave . . ."

"Nobody is off-limits," he said with a smile. "Not his momma, not his business, not his pretty little wife, not your law degree."

Yarni knew she hadn't done anything unethical, but she also knew she had pressed the envelope more times than she could remember to get her clients off. She wondered what he knew, or thought he knew.

She was sure he could see her wheels turning. "And I almost forgot." He picked up a photo of little Desi and kissed it.

That's all it took for Yarni to flip. "Nigga, you going to do something to a little kid? Are you really that fucked-up for real?" she asked with anger in her eyes. Once he threatened her sweet little Desi, she lost control and realized they were at the point of no return. That their destiny had already been dealt, and the cards would fall where they may.

"Just wanted you to know this shit here is like Afghanistan and ain't nobody safe. It's beef. It's war."

She walked toward him. "Get the fuck out. Coming here with idle threats. Who the fuck do you think you are?" she asked. Yarni looked at Cook'em-up like he was shit and didn't blink or back down.

"I forgot behind that law degree and that fancy suit, you's a real gangsta-type bitch, huh? You should've been on my team."

"You ain't a cat, nigga! You don't have nine lives. You bleed just like other bitches! You gonna come in here and threaten me and my child? You a pussy! Why ain't you face Des? We both know why: because you's a bitch-ass nigga, sucking other niggas' dick."

That last comment looked like it made Cook'em-up almost lose it. He raised his hand and she picked up a three-ring hole punch to let him know that if he hit her, then he better be prepared to take a hit back.

Yarni wished that she had her gun inside the office, not in her car, because she would have shot him dead on the spot. But then she thought again and realized he wasn't worth it.

"I see you are a little worked up. I just came to give you fair warning."

"Say yo' prayers, you rat bastard," Yarni screamed at the top of her lungs, and Layla rushed into her office. Cook'em-up smirked and walked out the door. Layla didn't know what was going on, although she had heard about this side of Yarni but never witnessed it for herself.

"Do I need to call 911?" Layla asked.

Yarni's eye caught the chessboard she had set up in her office and tried to regain her composure. She'd heard loud and clear what Cook'em-up had said, and to the best of her knowledge he was not one for making idle threats. From what she had heard, he was a man of action. At that second, she realized that this was all a chess game. Cook'em-up had delivered his message to force Des to make a move. But what Cook'em-up didn't know was that in chess, it wasn't the king who controlled the board—it was the queen. She was the most powerful player, and she always protected her king.

23

Giving Back to
the Game

Des's old friend Carson was in town and had called him for a
meeting. They had known each other since Des was eighteen
years old and over the years what started out as a business relationship had grown into a friendship. They decided to meet at a
sushi restaurant on the National Harbor in DC.

Initially when Carson called, Des had no idea why he wanted
to meet with him. A little over a year ago, Carson had approached Des about one last good, hard run, after which they
could both kiss the game good-bye, but Des had to respectfully
decline the offer because he already had his hands full with the
church and his own side hustles.

The entire time over lunch they were basically catching up,
and reminiscing over the good times they'd had over the years,
which had Des puzzled that that was all Carson had to talk to

him about. On one hand, it was good for Des to just take a breather, escape to the old days and not have to focus on what was going on in his world. But on the other, Des never lived his life looking in the rearview mirror. He liked to keep his eye on the road and right now any time away from his real world, not on the hunt for the people wanting his demise, was a minute wasted.

"Man, did you hear that a few of my major moneymaking spots got hit, including the one where I lay my head sometimes?"

"Naw, man," Des said. "I swear, it must be something in the air."

"Turns out the nigga that been getting me was a young punk, not even twenty years old," Carson said.

"Damn, they getting younger and bolder, huh?" Des said, shaking his head.

"I came eye to eye, just waiting for the right time to kill him."

Des nodded, thinking of what he'd do if he'd caught the people who were behind his misfortunes. He wasn't sure exactly how it would go, but one thing he knew was that the bastards who robbed him and tried to take his life from him would be dead.

"So, you got any leads on who got you?" Carson asked.

"Not yet, but I'm burning the streets up trying to get to the bottom of this."

"How's the wife?" Carson asked, abruptly changing the subject.

"She's being wifey. Just called, as a matter of fact. You know, she's always holding it down. They say behind every hustler stands a strong woman. She's mine."

"Who'd thought that the young girl who was a wild card would be the one always by your side?" Carson said. "And how's the baby girl?"

"She's good." Des smiled. "She's my little genius."

"I was shocked to find out that you had a grown daughter."

"Where did you hear that?" Des was surprised and wondered where Carson had gotten that information. He hadn't shared it with anyone outside his circle, and for a second he wondered if Carson was a part of the conspiracy against him.

"Long story."

"Well, share it over dessert." Des wanted to know why Carson would wait until the end of their meal to mention it.

He saw Carson tense up as he began to tell the story. "Apparently your daughter's boyfriend, Fame, robbed three different people who were all connected to me. If I didn't know any better, I would say that you sent them, but I know you didn't," he said with a tense smile.

Des leaned back in his chair and crossed his arms. He stared at Carson as he kept on with his story.

"With the help of your daughter, this Fame character dressed up like a broad and robbed the front man of my strip club."

"Really?" Des had figured that Desember was into some bullshit but had no idea it was this heavy.

"According to my people, apparently she was only there to watch his back, but when she thought he was in trouble, she came to her man's rescue and laid both guys down, tied 'em up and had them scared for their lives. Now that I know her pedigree, they had great reason to be."

Des nodded his head. He'd always wanted a son, and with the

kind of stunts that Desember had pulled off, she was like the son he never had. Des knew that Carson was a heinous man and his methods of revenge were extreme, and though he wasn't afraid—he feared no one but God—he really didn't need a war with Carson at this point in his life. "Let me apologize for my daughter's actions and—"

Carson cut him off. "Don't worry, she's in no danger. As a favor to you, I'm sparing your daughter's life. But that favor doesn't extend to that pussy-ass motherfucker who stole from me." Carson took a deep breath. "And gangsta to gangsta, you should be able to respect that."

"I do." Des nodded.

"As if getting away scot-free with my money wasn't enough, a few days later the son of a bitch was bold enough to come to one of the places where I lay my head and look me in the eye and tell me that he didn't care about the consequences of stealing from me." Carson was still pissed that Fame had told him this to his face.

"Clearly the young fella didn't know who he was dealing with," Des suggested. "He couldn't have known."

Carson took a deep breath. "You are right, he didn't know."

"Well, my man, you know everybody wasn't sat down and given the rules of the game like we were. And it's up to us—not just as old g's, but true g's—to pass the game along." Des knew he had Carson's attention. "I don't know the youngin—never met him before a day in my life—but apparently he got the game fucked up. I don't know why."

"He got it real fucked up," Carson agreed with Des.

"But can I make a suggestion?" Des asked.

"I've never stopped you before."

"Maybe instead of killing him there are some other drastic measures that could be taken."

"Like what?" Carson was hell-bent on killing Fame, but respected Des enough to hear him out.

"Like I said, I never met the lil homey, but from what you saying he seems good at what he does. So make 'im pay back the money, take him under your wing, show him the game, and he'll be in debt to you." Des ran it down like it was common sense. "If he has any kind of morals, he'll reciprocate it and be loyal to you. From what little I know about my daughter, I don't think she would be involved with anyone who didn't have any. But again, intellect and emotions are two different things."

"True."

Des knew Carson was considering what he said, so he continued. "If the guy has any kind of principles, you got you a lil soldier who feels he owes you his life, and he'll be loyal. You can use his skills to the best of your advantage." Des knew that Carson was partially sold. "But the sweetest part is that you'll find out how he was able to tap into your spots. You'll discover who is disloyal in your army."

"But I tried to kill him. Nobody forgives the man who tried to kill him. This could backfire."

"You tried to kill him and your guy missed. It's taboo for you to try again. There are no mistakes when it comes to divine intervention." Des noticed that he sounded like the pastor he'd been pretending to be but he kept going. "There is a reason," Des mentioned, "Fame is alive after your guy unloaded a clip in him. Also, he knows now that you can touch him anytime you want to, but you haven't. You know there comes a point in this life for niggas like us who have been through the fire branded by the game that we have to give back." Des shrugged. "It's the law of physics: you can't give shit to the universe and expect sugar back. You have to sometimes give sugar to keep your flow of sugar coming."

Carson grabbed the check off the table and peeled off a few bills to take care of it. "You definitely paid for the meal with your food for thought, so I'll pay for the food."

"I appreciate it, man. I gotta get back to my war zone before something else erupts," Des said, getting up from the table.

"So one favor deserves the next: I spared Desember and now you have to be the mediator between this Fame and me."

"Give me some time." Des chuckled as he wondered what in the hell else didn't he know about his daughter.

24

The Bombshell

Des walked away from the meeting with Carson feeling optimistic and was thinking that he couldn't wait to get home to see his daughters, but mainly his wife. He made a mental note that he had to start sending Yarni flowers, but more, he had to stop taking their quality time together for granted. His thoughts prompted him to call Yarni as he walked to his car.

When she answered, he started singing, "I Just Called to Say I Love You," by Stevie Wonder.

He could feel her smile through the phone, and knew she was about to join in with him, when she received another call and said it was probably the news she had been waiting on. "Hold on real quick, baby, let me see why Layla is calling after hours. Give me one second to make sure she is all right."

Layla asked if Yarni was sitting down. After Yarni assured her that she was, her assistant dropped a bombshell on her: she had the name of the person who received the call from Roxanne's cell phone.

Yarni was dumbfounded by what she heard and wondered why she hadn't put two and two together herself. She couldn't click back over to the other line fast enough to tell Des what she'd discovered.

"Babe," she said to Des, "you ain't gonna believe this shit."

"You ain't gonna believe this either," he said into his Bluetooth. "I'm surrounded by the Feds!"

That was the last thing she heard him say before the phone went dead.

The Feds

It didn't matter if they were from the DEA, FBI, ATF or IRS; Des hated all the alphabet boys with a passion. In his opinion they were arrogant and overrated. They loved to throw around the fact that they had a ninety percent plus conviction rate, but failed to mention that they wouldn't know jackshit if it wasn't for cowardly, cheese-eating rats telling on anybody to save their own ass.

"You've done quite well for yourself, Mr. Desmond Taylor," said Barnes, the agent who appeared to be in charge. He was tall and gaunt, wearing a cheap gray suit and loafers with rubber soles that squeaked. Des counted six Feds. He recognized four of them—they'd been inside of his gym when he was working out.

"Shit!" Des cursed, disappointed in himself for not penning the spooks earlier. "If you don't mind taking that bullshit off of my phone, I'd like to call my lawyer," Des politely stated. They used some kind of device to shut off the connection to Des's cell phone.

"That won't be necessary, Mr. Taylor, or can I call you Des?" Agent Barnes asked. "This isn't that type of confrontation. You are not under arrest and we are not here to take you away."

Des remained silent, deciding to listen rather than talk.

"We've had you under investigation for the last eighteen months. And I can tell you one thing," the Fed said as if he was an admirer of Des, "you are one smooth customer. That bogus church you are running is perfectly legal and was an ingenious idea for washing your dirty money. Nothing new, but brilliant all the same." He nodded as if he was congratulating Des, but Des wasn't falling for it.

He told the agent straight-up, "If it's all right with you, I can do without the smoke being blown up my ass. If you got something to say, go ahead and say it."

"As I was saying," Agent Barnes continued, unfazed by the interruption, "you're good at what you do. We know you are still dirty but no one is willing to finger you—at least not on the stand. But it's only a matter of time. Unless . . ."

"I guess that's my cue," Des said. "Okay, I'll play along. Unless what?"

Agent Barnes beamed a wide, arrogant smile. "During our surveillance of you we discovered that Detective Columbo of the RPD has gone completely rogue: murder, drugs, prostitution, extortion—we want him off the street, but we don't have enough physical evidence to get a conviction."

"And what does that have to do with me?"

"If you take the stand and say that Chris Weathers, also known as Cook'em-up, told you that Columbo paid him and supplied him with the weaponry to try to kill you, then rob your church and shoot your homeboy Tony, we may be convinced to turn a blind eye to you as long as you stay away from the violent stuff."

This was almost too much information to digest at one time, Des thought. He could stick it to a cop that had been a pain in the ass since he made his first "big eight" sale, and get a free pass from the Feds. All he had to do was flush everything he stood for down the toilet.

He looked at the agent and he could read that Barnes was sure he had Des cornered.

"Agent Barnes," the Fed was all ears, "that's a mighty compelling offer," he said.

"Isn't it? I think it is the deal of a lifetime." Agent Barnes obviously figured he had Des exactly where he wanted him.

Des nodded with a smile. "For a chump. And Joyce Taylor didn't raise no chumps or snitches. Pig or rat, snitching is snitching."

Agent Barnes shook his head. "There won't be another offer."

Des knew that they would come after him even more than before, but what could he do? He had his rules and they had theirs.

"Good," he said. "Then I guess this lil ambush meeting is over?"

Agent Barnes replied, "For now."

26

A Girl's Gotta Do

After calling Des's attorney right away to give him a heads-up, Yarni's mind began to run wild as she drove down the highway replaying her brief conversation with Des and the confrontation with Cook'em-up in her head and as she thought about the reality of the situation.

She wanted to call Bambi, but at that moment everyone was suspect. Even her trust for her sister was in question, because Bambi was married to Lynx, and Cook'em-up was Lynx's right-hand man, Bambi and Lynx were broke, and Yarni knew that Lynx had asked Des for a drug connect, but Des had put it on the back burner. She wondered if Lynx and Cook'em-up were in cahoots together. And if Bambi knew anything. For as long as Yarni knew her, Bambi hadn't dated anyone other than Lynx, and they did have a child together. Yes, Yarni and Bambi had the same father, but what did that mean really? They hadn't grown up together, and had only found out they were sisters a few years ago. Their relationship was more like best friends than sisters, and she hated that she had to raise the question of who Bambi would be more loyal to: her husband or her sister.

Yarni's thoughts were interrupted by Tupac's "Dear Momma" ring tone. It was her mother. Even though she was caught up in her own drama, she needed to make sure that Gloria was okay and that she wasn't a target of any of this ongoing madness too. That was the last thing her mother needed. Though tears rolled down her face, Yarni tried to keep her pain out of her voice so her mother wouldn't notice. "Hey, Ma, what's up?"

"Oh nothing much," her mother said, sounding as if she was in high spirits.

"Aren't we in a good mood today."

"Yes, I am. I have a quick question for you. Do you know of or could you find me a good divorce attorney here in Florida?"

"Mom, why don't you wait until you are finished with your radiation? Is Sam still showing his butt?"

"No, he isn't. Actually, he's been on his best behavior around here, waiting on me hand and foot. But it's just the thought that he'd cheat on me, period, while I have cancer. That put the nail in the coffin.

"You know I'm on all kinds of meds and they have side effects. And God forbid I wake up one day and have a flashback and kill his ass. So I'm going to be the bigger person and get this no-good son of a bitch out of my life the easy way so I don't have to give him a first-class ticket to Hell."

Yarni admired how strong her mother was even as she fought

cancer, and knew that's the type of person her mother had raised her to be. "Mommy, you make me so proud."

"You think just because I'm sick I'm going to let a man treat me any kind of way? I don't need him to feel any pity on me. Please, chile, under the most harsh circumstances and through the most intense heartache and pain, I always taught you that a girl's gotta do what a girl's gotta do. And guess what? I'm going to do what I have to do."

"That's right, Mommy!" Yarni smiled. Even though her mother didn't call her intending to give her the power that she needed at that very moment in her own life, that is just what she'd done. Her mother somehow always knew the right words to say to Yarni, exactly when she needed to hear them. Yarni was convinced that Gloria was more than her mother. She was her guardian angel.

"I will have to do some research for you, but give me a couple of days to find you the perfect lawyer. I'll check on you later."

As soon as she disconnected, the words "a girl's gotta do what a girl's gotta do" reverberated through her head. She was already en route to meet Des at home. She would explain everything to him in person.

Yarni knew that all eyes were on Des, and for the sake of her family she had to take the matter into her own hands. She grabbed her cell phone, called the only two people other than her mother and Des she knew with all her heart and soul she could trust with her life: her uncle Stanka and her father. She arranged to meet with them. Her next call was to Joyce.

"Shit is too complicated to explain. Just listen to me. Go get

Desi from school and watch after her 'til you hear from me or Des."

Joyce didn't like being left out of the loop but she agreed.

Yarni filled Stanka and her father in on what Cook'em-up said and they knew that Yarni was serious. She wasn't one to ever cry wolf. They assured her that they were on top of it.

Yarni just hoped and prayed that it wasn't too late.

27

Gut Feeling

When Des finally arrived home, he poured himself a stiff drink. He heard something behind him and turned around.

"Oh Dad, it's you," Desember said, relieved as she held a gun by her side. It still felt strange; her calling him Dad and him answering to it.

"Put that shit away. What the fuck you doing with a gun?" he asked.

"Relax, I know how to use it. Fame showed me so I've been thoroughly trained."

Des was about to ask if she thought she was Ms. Rambo or something but Desember kept talking.

"And besides, Yarni called frantic and said stuff was serious and for me to stay here and if I heard anything to shoot first and ask questions later."

Des reached for the house phone to try to call Yarni. "How long ago has it been since you spoke with her?" Once the Feds had let him go he'd thrown his cell phone in the river.

"About an hour."

Yarni answered, relieved, and told him to stay put, that shit had hit the fan and she was on her way home. When he disconnected from her, Des paced the floor.

"Where were you, Des?" she asked.

"Saving your life and trying to negotiate a cost for your knucklehead boyfriend's life."

"What are you talking about?" Desember asked.

"You disobeyed everybody: me, your mother, your stepmother, even your boyfriend when you and Lava went back to North Carolina."

"Lava had nothing to do with it," she said. "She was there to watch my back."

"Well, she didn't do a good job because as soon as you got to the hospital, you were followed back here, and the man that was responsible for Fame's shooting did some research and connected the dots that I was your father. The man, the one Fame robbed, happens to be a good friend of mine."

Desember's face brightened up. "Well, since this person is your friend, can Fame just pay him back the money that he owes him and promise never to rob anyone else again?"

"It's not that simple," Des told his daughter. "Plus it's in him. You know he can't stop robbing."

"He can. People change," she said with a straight face. She knew Des was a smart man, and she was trying to say whatever she could to persuade her father to help keep Fame alive.

"Look, don't bullshit your father," Des told her.

"But I really think he's learned his lesson. Please help!" she pleaded.

Des was quiet. This was not the life that he had in mind for any daughter of his. He never wanted his daughter to be with a robber and a thief, but he knew he couldn't control who his daughter loved. As he thought deeper from a father's perspective, to really shield his daughter from all the heartbreaks of being a hustler's wife, he should go kill Fame himself.

He was torn: should he take Fame under his wing, and raise and watch over him the way he wished he would have raised Nasir? Maybe taking on Fame would fill the guilty void of how he'd turned his nephew on to his friend and Colombian drug connection Rico, which ultimately cost Nasir his life. It was definitely something to think about.

"Dad, if you do this for me, I will be forever grateful. And I will do anything you say." She tried to bribe him.

"Is that right?"

"I swear."

"Relax, I'm already trying to work out the details."

She gave him a hug and uttered the two words she had longed to say to her real father her entire life, "Thanks, Dad." Then added, "You won't be sorry, I promise!"

He smiled. "No, but cut me a piece of that chocolate cake." He pointed to the cake that was in the clear stand displayed on the counter.

"A'ight, no problem." She grabbed a small plate to put it on.

As she was cutting the cake the memory of something that had been gnawing at her for a few days saddened her mood. At first she thought telling Des would make him look at her like a child with an overactive imagination. But she couldn't shake the feeling.

"Dad," she said—each time the endearments rolled off her tongue it felt more natural—"I don't know if this means anything, but I don't like that dude Cook'em-up."

Des was puzzled. "What type of dealings you had with him that it concerns your personal feelings," he asked.

"I met him one day at Rocko's house. Ever since we resolved our situation we got into, we been spending lots of time together." She put the cake on the plate.

This was the first time that Desember had mentioned Rocko's name around Des. Yarni had filled him in on the ordeal, but father and daughter hadn't talked about it. There had been a lot going on for everyone.

Turning up his face, Des questioned, "How close?"

He can't be thinking what I think he thinking, she thought. "Uggh! Not that close, Dad." Now her face twisted. "I got good taste when it comes to guys."

"That's a relief," Des said, trying not to get worked up at the thought that his daughter was entertaining the offspring of his enemy.

"We are mad cool—brother/sister type of cool."

Des made it clear: "Well, he ain't yo' brother."

"You know what I mean; how about like cousins, then?" she asked.

Before Des could answer, they heard a car in the driveway slam on its breaks, probably making skid marks on the pavement.

A moment later Yarni put her key in the door.

"Baby luv?" Des called out to her. "We in here." Then he focused his attention back on Desember. "Now, what about you? Trying to sleep with the enemy."

"It ain't nothing like that, when I went to meet up with Rocko about some business, we ran into Cook'em-up. I know he's supposed to be Aunt Bambi's husband's friend, but something isn't right about that dude."

Des remained quiet. Listening closely.

"Something about him gave me the creeps. I could feel it deep in my gut; I don't think he likes you either," Desember came right out and said. "When he found out I was your daughter, he gave me a vile look. He tried to hide it fast but his eyes kept giving it away."

Yarni chimed in. "She's right, Des."

With every syllable Yarni used to describe the surreal encounter she had had with Cook-'em-up while at work, Des's blood ascended to a torrid pitch.

He wasn't sure if Cook'em-up had a death wish, but whether he did or not, Des was sure that by the morning Cook'em-up would wish he was never born.

28

Papa Was a
Rolling Stone

The minute Yarni was done filling Des in, her "Papa Was a Rolling Stone" ringtone went off. Lloyd let it be known that he was on his way over with valuable information and instructed them to stay put.

When he arrived, he got right to the point. "Look, man, you hotter than fish grease at a New Orleans cookout. You gotta fall back and let the old-timers handle this."

"Man, you ain't no killer, you a bank robber." Des wasn't trying to hear this. "No disrespect, Lloyd, but you got your rep taking money, not lives."

Lloyd held his ground. "We do this my way, and if anything goes wrong I'll take the rap. The son of a bitch threatened my daughter and granddaughter. Let me do this for you. You'll be doing me a favor letting me handle it—my plan, my score to settle, my soldiers."

Des wanted to remind him that it was *his* wife and daughters; his beef, but this wasn't the time for a family argument. Lloyd was not only stuck in the seventies, he was stuck in his ways.

Instead, Des spoke strategy. "If he went to see Yarni today, you know he's calculated this. He won't be out in the street waiting to be knocked off. He's dumb," Des said, "but not that dumb."

"He expects for us to run out like madmen searching the streets," Lloyd agreed. "My plan is to make him come to me."

Easier said than done, Des thought.

He studied his father-in-law's eyes. They were devoid of emotion. "And how do you propose to execute this plan of yours?" Des wanted to know.

Smiling, Lloyd picked an apple from the fruit bowl on the kitchen island and wiped it off with a paper towel. "I know where his grandmother lives. I plan on him being a good grandson."

Des didn't like it. Sounded too familiar.

"It's too close to the stunt he tried to pull when he sent the kid to my mother's house. Too predictable," Des surmised.

"That's exactly the reason why I think it'll work," Lloyd said, then paused.

Des waited for Lloyd to finish.

"What makes it unpredictable," Lloyd said, "is that he will never expect you to perpetrate a move he's already made. It's the last thing he'd think to see from you."

For the first time in a while, Des cracked a smile. More like a half smirk.

Sometimes simplicity was best. And this simple plan was lucid enough to work.

29

Live by the Sword

Bernice Weathers soundly slept in her pink sponge rollers and light green nightgown, unaware of the masked men creeping into her house at three o'clock in the morning. The men were heavily armed and quietly searched the small home to be sure that she was the only person there before waking her up gently, by tapping her shoulder with a gun.

Bernice awakened and although her sight wasn't what it used to be, she couldn't miss the giant gun barrel that sat on the edge of her nose. The woman damn near had a heart attack once she realized it wasn't a dream but a real gun in her face.

"Oh Lord, please Lord! Help! Don't take me now. Don't take me like this!"

"He ain't the one you need to call, Ms. Weathers," Lloyd said from behind his ski mask. "If you don't want to die, you need to call your grandson and get him here."

"I don't have anything to do with that good-for-nothing scoundrel." Bernice guessed what these men had planned for her grandson and she probably should feel sorry for him, but she didn't. Chris "Cook'em-up" Weathers had never been a good person. He was a jealous-hearted, selfish child who grew into an even meaner teenager. By the time he was seventeen he was a full-blown monster who didn't give a damn about anybody but himself. He killed for money, and God only knew what else.

Bernice recited a silent prayer before saying, "I need my glasses to get his number out of my phone book."

Lloyd handed the lady her glasses from the night table. With her bifocals in place her vision cleared and she saw three more men in her bedroom, also holding big guns. "Do you mind passing me my housecoat because I don't want to let it all hang out and alarm anybody."

Lloyd did as the old lady asked. After putting on her robe she located Cook'em-up's phone number and dialed the digits on her old-fashioned rotary phone.

Des stood in the shadows by the door. The lady was living in a time capsule, he thought to himself. There was an old television set with rabbit ears attached, outdated appliances in the kitchen, and old furniture that should have been thrown out twenty years ago. It was obvious that the lady was living on a fixed income and hadn't benefited from any of the luxuries that Cook'em-up could have afforded his own grandmother.

Bernice's hands were shaking so hard it was difficult for her to dial. It seemed like it took forever. Lloyd reminded her, "It is not our intention to hurt you, ma'am."

"Don't worry; I won't give you a reason to. I'm going to do as you ask of me," she said, finally able to complete dialing. Bernice looked up at him with humility in her face as if she could see through the mask. "It's ringing," she said with hope in her voice. Then after a few moments, she sighed and hung up the phone. "He didn't answer."

Bernice was terrified of what might happen next, being that she couldn't contact that fool of a grandson of hers.

Lloyd tried to calm her down some. "Don't panic. We'll just sit here for a few and then you can try him again," he said. "We're not in a hurry."

Two minutes later, to everyone's surprise, the old phone rang. It sounded like a school fire alarm. "Hello? I'm doing just awful," she faked a cough. "I need you to get my prescription filled for me at the twenty-four-hour CVS. I need it tonight! If I don't get 'em you may be burying me in the morning," she exaggerated. "I feel just horrible." She sounded convincing. "I need my medications right now."

"Damn, Grandma, can't it wait until in the morning?" the dirty bastard on the other end of the phone asked.

"I'm an eighty-five-year-old woman, and you're leaving me to die," Bernice protested.

Des was on the phone in the living room, listening to the conversation to make sure she wasn't sending Cook'em-up any coded messages, and as far as he could tell, she wasn't.

The guilt trip worked.

"I'm on my way, Grandma." Bernice heard her grandson swear under his breath before hanging up.

Lloyd instructed her to get dressed. She modestly pulled a sweat suit over her nightgown before sitting down to wait, praying her grandson wouldn't let her down.

Cook'em-up must've not been into anything too serious, because twenty minutes later he was putting a key in his grandmother's front door lock, letting himself in. Before he knew what hit him, he was snatched up and cracked across the back of his skull with a heavy pistol before his foot could touch the thirty-year-old threadbare carpet covering his grandmother's floor.

"Oh shit!" He grunted both from the shock of the situation he was in and the pain from the head blow. "What the fuck is going on?"

His grandmother refused to let her last words to him be a lie. "You disgust me," she said, "and this world would probably be a better place without you. You live by the sword, you die by the sword."

Des took Bernice out of the house, put her into a car and drove her to a hotel. "I apologize, ma'am, for interrupting your beauty rest." He gave her ten one-hundred-dollar bills, then hoping that she had insurance on the boy but figuring she probably didn't, he dug in his pocket and gave her everything he had. "Don't waste one penny burying that fool. Treat yourself to whatever it is that your heart desires," he instructed her.

She nodded and asked, "Can I go now?"

"Yes, you can—and remember, we're still going to be watching you, so leave the police out of this."

Des pulled away and took off the mask. He was calling it a night, heading home to be with his wife and daughters.

30

Rock Hard

At a construction site on the outskirts of town, Lloyd and the old-timers were having a little fun. At first they used torture tactics on Cook'em-up that would have been frowned upon if done to the prisoners at Guantanamo Bay. Cook'em-up was praying that they would hurry and kill him.

A funnel was stuffed into his mouth and cement was poured slowly down his throat a little at a time. As Cook'em-up was forced to drink the concrete, Lloyd smoked a cigarette and watched with a smile. "So it wasn't enough that you had gotten away with what I'm guessing—with all the players you had in place—was close to or more than half a million dollars from whatever role you played in the robbery of the church?" Lloyd took another pull of the Newport. "That just wasn't enough, huh? You should have packed a bag and left the city, at least that's what any smart man with as much blood as you have on your hands would have done."

"He ain't smart," Johnny, the stocky old head holding the funnel said. He and Lloyd's friendship started over forty years ago in a juvenile dormitory.

"Yeah, then you go fuck with my daughter. You ain't seriously thinking there wasn't going to be any repercussions, were you?" Lloyd looked at Cook'em-up's face, which wore a look of terror.

Cook'em-up wanted to beg the man to shoot him, to get it over with, but the cement was beginning to clog his vocal cords. Lloyd read the utter despair in Cook'em-up's eyes and felt no pity.

"Ain't no need to beg, nigga. None at all.

"You not only went to my daughter's office and fucked up her workday, but you had to shoot threats at my granddaughter too. What happened to a man's woman and children being off-limits?" With a slight chuckle, he shook his head. "You got shit really fucked-up."

Lloyd eyeballed Cook'em-up and saw the look of death.

A broken, desperate man was always a pitiful sight, and Cook'em-up was no different.

"None of this was my idea," he croaked to Lloyd and who-ever else would listen. "I was just a pawn. Everything was so obvious, but Des couldn't figure it all out. If I tell you who was really after him, will you promise to kill me quickly?"

"You ain't in no position to make no deals, but I guess it depends on the song you sing."

Cook-'em-up had no illusions about living, no matter what he told them, but he couldn't think of anything worse than being buried alive, encased in rock, so he sung like the choir at the Good Life Ministry.

Even Lloyd was surprised when Cook'em-up spilled the beans, and hated that he had to break the news that one of Des's trusty sixpack was in on it.

Lloyd took one last long pull of his cigarette and blew the smoke in Cook'em-up's face. "You ready to get this shit over with, man?"

With tears in his eyes, Cook'em-up nodded. Lloyd put the cigarette out in his face. "A'ight, y'all," he said to his partners in crime.

The old heads walked Cook'em-up over to what looked like a predug ditch in the middle of what would later be the parking lot of the new superstore in the process of being built. They threw him in like he was a rag doll. Cook'em-up was so worn down that he could barely try to escape, even when Johnny hit the button for the concrete to pour on him. When Johnny stopped it, it was only up to Cook'em-up's knees. Though it was hopeless, the hit man scrummed for about two hours.

The fellas laughed at him and cracked jokes as if he was their form of entertainment. Johnny hit it again and brought the concrete up to Cook'em-up's neck. That sat for another two hours and Cook'em-up was delirious by then, and that's when Lloyd said, "Since this is the last thing you will ever hear in this lifetime, I hope in the next one, you will remember never to fuck with a real gangsta's family." Lloyd spit on him. "We done wasted enough of our golfing time on this sack of shit! Put the motherfucker out of his misery."

31

Breaking the Cycle

Now the cat was out of the bag that Chip—one of their oldest and once dearly trusted friends, and treasurer for the church—was one of the masterminds behind the robbery of the Good Life Ministry. Though the jury was still out on who the other one was, for now Chip would have to take responsibility for Tony's death during the heist. There was no doubt that Black Bob wanted to make good on his word and was planning to get the name of his partner while at it. And Des and Slim swore on the graves of their loved ones to take care of Chip's unknown partner if it was the last thing they did.

While Des was with Slim and Black Bob having a drink now that things were finally coming together, the three girls were homebound.

Desember had been keeping Desi busy while Yarni was trying

to get some work done. She decided to take a break and go downstairs for a snack, but as she reached the family room, she listened to Desember playing with Desi. The short time that her stepdaughter had been with them, Yarni had gotten used to her being there. Though Desember had her moments, she was really good with Desi.

"I want to be just like you when I grow up," Desi said to her big sister.

Yarni cringed. Desember had grown on her and she was confident that with the right guidance the girl would go on to do some great things, but where Desember was at that very moment in her life wasn't what Yarni had in mind for her daughter, she thought as she continued to observe her daughter looking up at Desember.

"No." Desember shook her head. "You don't want to be like me; you have to be better than me."

"But we are sisters and we're supposed to be alike," Desi said.

Yarni smiled and thought how blessed the girls were, especially Desi—she had two parents that loved her and an adoring big sister.

Then she noticed that Desi had gotten quiet as if she was thinking something. Apparently Desember noticed it too. "What's on your mind, small puffs?" she asked.

"My friend Morgan, who's in my class. She has three big sisters, and if somebody messes with her, she always brags and says her sisters are going to come to our school and beat them up. Is it true that big sisters can come to school and beat people up their little sisters hate?"

"You betta believe it," Desember said, picking up Desi. "Tell me who's messing with my baby sister." She leaned down and started tying Desi's shoes. "I'll go up there and stomp," she stomped the floor with her foot, "them like they're a roach."

Desi smiled, obviously happy that her sister had her back, then told Desember her problem. "Well, this boy named Chauncey said that my momma and daddy are gangsters and so I'm going to grow up to be one."

Yarni damn near choked as she listened to her daughter worry about growing up to be a gangster. "When I asked my teacher what a gangster was, she said bad people. So I hate Chauncey and I put paint on his favorite chair when nobody was looking, so when movie time came, he sat in it. And everybody was laughing but nobody saw me doing it because it was dark," Desi said matter-of-factly.

"Give me five." Desember put her hand up. "That's my little sister!"

Desi gave her five. "But I still want you to come to my school and stomp," she stomped her foot, "him like the roachie bug he is."

Yarni overheard the entire conversation and it broke her heart.

What the hell was she thinking? This life they were living wasn't what she wanted for her daughter. A couple of years ago Desi had been kidnapped—maybe she was too young to remember. Now she had to protect herself from schoolkids who call her parents gangsters.

Tears came to Yarni's eyes as she thought about the reality of it, that all the people Desi looked up to were gangsta: Des, Desember, Joyce, Lloyd, Bambi—well, she was borderline but could get real gully. And although Yarni hated to admit it, in her own way she was gangsta too. If she wasn't, she was damn sure a gangsta's wife.

When she was younger, she thought being a hustler's wife was all fun and games. She went on to be an attorney and changed her life for the better, but when needed, she could slip back into that mind-set. She knew she had to put herself under construction and renovate her lifestyle and principles.

She had to ask herself what kind of life she was living. She could defend people tooth and nail, and saw how dirty the system was, but then she would come home and partake in the same life she got people off the hook for.

She had to admit how twisted and fucked-up it was.

Yarni knew firsthand that the life she and Des were living was dysfunctional. Desi didn't deserve having to live this way nor did she want that for her child.

It was a means to no end, and one day their luck would run out. One day it wouldn't be a brush with death, it would be death. And one day God would have no mercy for them.

Everything had to, and would, come to end . . . tonight!

Des would have to pick—it was either the streets or the sheets. Their family or the gangsta life.

No more flipflopping or riding the fence. No more of dreams of the last, the greatest or the ultimate hustle.

Enough was enough! It was time for her to put her foot down—and whatever the repercussions were, she'd take it on the chin.

She fully understood, without a reasonable doubt, what was at stake.

Tonight Yarni would give Des an ultimatum. Though she couldn't bet on the outcome, she knew one thing: tonight her life would change, *forever!*

Acknowledgments

I must thank God, whom through all blessings flow. He keeps blessing me over and over and over again with great people who have impacted my life and have my back time after time, day after day!

My dear children, I do it for you! I'm so proud that you are mine! I love you. My family and small circle of real friends . . . I thank you

Special thanks to: Craig for always having my back no matter what. Tim Patterson, thanks for always having the words to keep me going on the rainy days and for the excitement on the sunny days. No words can express my gratitude on those days. Mia Upshaw, for those words of encouragement and for having such compassion through all the craziness. Wanda David, for your love and support, always wanting the best for me. Natakiki, for your laughs and perspective. Auntie Yvonne, for always having a solution and knowing what to say to make me feel better! My little cousin, Natalee; so glad we are so close. Alyce- Nikki Allen, I love you for your concern. Trevenia Blancher, I thank you for all those days that you drove to the country to bring me food or ran errands and just your overall ride or die love in general. Noel, the sky is the limit. Dr. Gregory Pleasants, for being on top of my health, for caring, not just for me but all your patients. You truly are the greatest! My chiropractor, Dr. Larry Griffin (Dr. G. Stacks), you are so passionate about your work; never change the way you are. Laura Cook, OMG!!! If those walls could share our laughs, the entire world would be laughing or shaking their heads at us. Carrie K, your hands are like butter. Thanks for the great massages.

Melody, I thank you for allowing me the opportunity to bring my thoughts to print and I truly value the bond we have outside of the pages. Marc, for assisting in taking my career to such heights and seeing outside the box when no one else does. I'm so happy for you and all the great things that are happening for you. You deserve it!

And the best thank-you is always last: to you, my loyal readers. I love you for loving me and my work! Thank YOU!!! for all the love and support!